THE BAD COMPANY

BAD COMPANY, BOOK 1

CRAIG MARTELLE

MICHAEL ANDERLE

THE BAD COMPANY TEAM

**JIT Beta Readers -
From each of us, our deepest gratitude!**

Maria Stanley

Leo Roars

Sherry Foster

Micky Cocker

Kelly ODonnell

Peter Manis

John Findlay

James Caplan

Kimberly Boyer

Tim Bischoff

Larry Omans

Sarah Weir

Thomas Ogden

Joshua Ahles

*If we missed anyone, **_please_** let us know!*

We can't write without those who support us
On the home front, we thank you for being there for us

We wouldn't be able to do this for a living if it weren't for our readers
We thank you for reading our books
-Craig and Michael

CHARACTERS & TIMELINE

Find the high-res version of the Kurtherian Timeline here: http://kurtherianbooks.com/timeline_jeff/

http://kurtherianbooks.com/timeline_jeff/

WORLD'S WORST DAY EVER (WWDE)

WWDE + 20 years, Terry Henry returns from self-imposed exile. The Terry Henry Walton Chronicles detail his adventures from that time to WWDE+150

WWDE + 150 years – Michael returns to earth. BA returns to earth. TH & Char go to Space

KEY PLAYERS

- **Terry Henry Walton** (was 45 on the WWDE) – called TH by his friends, Enhanced with nanocytes by Bethany Anne herself (now

Empress of the Federation), wears the rank of Colonel, leads the Force de Guerre (FDG), a military unit that he established on WWDE+20

- **Charumati** (was 65 on the WWDE) – A Werewolf, married to Terry, carries the rank of Major in the FDG
- **Kimber** (born WWDE+15, adopted approximately WWDE+25 by TH & Char, enhanced on WWDE+65) – Major in the FDG
- Her husband **Auburn Weathers** (enhanced on WWDE+82) – provides logistics support to the FDG
- **Kaeden** (born WWDE+16, adopted approximately WWDE+24 by TH & Char, enhanced on WWDE+65) – Major in the FDG
- His wife **Marcie Spires** (born on WWDE+22, naturally enhanced) – Colonel in the FDG
- **Cory** (born WWDE+25, naturally enhanced, gifted with the power to heal)
- Her husband **Ramses** (born WWDE+23, enhanced on WWDE+65) – Major in the FDG

VAMPIRES

- Joseph (born 300 years before the WWDE)
- Petricia (Born WWDE+30)

PRICOLICI (WEREWOLVES THAT WALK UPRIGHT)

- Nathan Lowell (President of the Bad Company and Bethany Anne's chief of intelligence)
- Ecaterina (Nathan's spouse)
- Christina (Nathan & Ecaterina's daughter

WEREWOLVES

- Sue and Timmons (long-term members of Char's pack)
- Shonna & Merrit (long term members of Char's pack)
- Ted (with Felicity, an enhanced human)

WERETIGERS BORN BEFORE THE WWDE

- Aaron & Yanmei

FORSAKEN

- Joseph (born 300 years before the WWDE)
- Petricia (born WWDE+30)

HUMANS (ENHANCED)

- Micky San Marino, Captain of the War Axe
- Commander Suresha, War Axe Department Head – Engines
- Commander MacEachthighearna (Mac), War Axe Department Head – Environmental
- Commander Blagun Lagunov, War Axe Department Head – Structure
- Commander Oscar Wirth, War Axe Department Head – Stores
- Lieutenant Clodagh Shortall, War Axe engine technician

OTHER KEY CHARACTERS

- Dokken (a sentient dog)
- The Good King Wenceslaus (an orange tabby who thinks he's a Weretiger, all fifteen pounds of him)
- K'thrall – a Yollin who works on the bridge of the War Axe

An explosion sounded and plasma fire flashed before his eyes.

Hidden in a remote corner of the Pan Galaxy, Nathan Lowell sat in his private office looking at the video communication screen. The President of the Bad Company frowned.

His Direct Action Branch was engaged and not in a good way. Nathan slowly shook his head as he watched.

Thirty-seven star systems away, General Lance Reynolds saw the same images displayed on his monitor. He chewed vigorously on his cigar. The report wasn't what he had expected.

Colonel Terry Henry Walton, the man in the image, looked back and forth between the screen and something to his left. Ominous sounds accompanied the image.

"This first mission wasn't what we contracted for, Nathan," Terry yelled at the portable console that sat with a sideways tilt. He stared at a point off-screen, shook his head, and continued. "My first stop when I get off this rock is that dandy president's office where I'll wring his pencil-neck to get our thirty percent bonus and seventy percent kicker. And then I'm leveling *his fucking palace!*"

"Can you settle this with what you have?" Lance asked.

"Yes, sir," Terry replied.

"I already told you once, call me Lance."

"No can do, General. Can't have you thinking I've grown soft just because I've been a pseudo-civilian for over a hundred and fifty years. Hang on." Terry's smile evaporated as he looked off-screen, his lip curling involuntarily. "SHOOT HIM!" he shouted.

The crack of hand-held railguns answered. Terry stabbed his finger at something neither Nathan nor Lance could see.

"Not that one, the *other* one," Terry corrected. More cracks from the hypervelocity weapons. Terry nodded and flipped the bird. "Fuck you, buddy, and your stupid-looking stalk-head!"

Terry turned back to the screen. "Where were we?"

"Something about you intending to level our client's palace," Nathan said coldly.

"After we're paid, that is. Hang on." Terry looked off-screen again, flinched with surprise, and started yelling, "Why won't you die? WOULD SOMEONE KILL THAT THING!"

Terry continued to watch off-screen.

A rapid barrage followed, then a brief silence, and finally a blast that nearly threw the colonel off his feet. Laughing, Terry brushed his uniform jacket with his free hand. "Come back from that one, you blue fuck!"

"Sorry, General, Nathan. There's about a hundred times more of these crawly bastards than we were led to believe. Mano-a-mano ain't working. For every one we pop, five more appear in its place. Gotta run. We need to lop the head off this dragon. Have your people call my people and we'll do lunch." Terry saluted and ran off-screen. Plasma beams cut through the spot where the colonel had just been standing.

"I'll call our least favorite client right now and tell him to stand the fuck by. I'm coming for a visit," Nathan growled, eyes flashing yellow as his anger charged his Were form. He tamped down the urge to change into a Pricolici, an upright-walking werewolf.

He didn't have the luxury of tearing up the universe. He was in charge and had passed the mantle of Bad Company door-kicker-in-chief to Terry Henry Walton.

Lance Reynolds stroked his chin as he thought about the man who looked happy to be in the middle of a battle seemingly raging out of control.

TERRY MADE mental notes of the battlefield as he ran from one position to another. He'd brought all six of the shuttle pods carrying the tactical teams, which still put his Direct Action Branch of the Bad Company in an inferior position.

"Run and gun. We need to run and gun!" Terry shouted at the angry red sky. He adjusted his helmet as it slipped backward. He worked his shoulders to loosen his ballistic vest too as he subconsciously considered a running battle, with rapid action and constant movement.

But they couldn't. They came under fire the second they ran off the drop ships. The shuttles had buttoned up and taken off immediately afterwards to hold a position out of range of the big guns. Or rockets. Or mortars.

Terry wasn't sure about the enemy's weapons, only caring about what he had to do to take them out. His tactical teams were made up of werewolves, weretigers, vampires, and enhanced humans. They had centuries of experience, and were best at making surgical strikes, small teams inserting behind enemy lines.

They weren't immortal, only enhanced by nanocytes, technology taken from Kurtherian scientists. They were still human, but *different*.

Terry would never say their enhancements made them better. He would say that their minds and their teamwork made them better. They believed that they trained hard to make war anticlimactic.

"Where's Kaeden with my mechs?" Terry shouted over the explosions.

Charumati, his purple-eyed werewolf wife, put a finger to her ear as she used her internal comm chip to talk with her son. Terry had a chip too, but he didn't want to lose focus on the battle as it raged on all sides of their position.

"This is the most fucked-up thing I've ever been a part of," he growled. He clenched his jaw. The muscles stood out of his face and a vein throbbed in his forehead. He carried a Jean Dukes Special pistol in one hand and his Mameluke sword in the other. The pistol was dialed to five out of a maximum of eleven.

"He's over the hill to the right. The fireworks you see are from his section," Char relayed.

"Can he get through their lines?"

Char's eyes unfocused for a moment, then she shook her head.

Terry slid his sword over his shoulder and into its scabbard strapped under his backpack. He took his pistol in both hands and dialed it to eleven. "Order a tactical retrograde to our position. We're breaking through right over there." Terry pointed to a heavily-wooded area covering the top of a hill.

"Joseph, where the hell are you?" Terry asked out loud, before switching to his comm chip. Powered by human energy, with a little extra boost from the Etheric dimension, the comm chips allowed the group to talk with each other. It also translated a vast number of human and alien languages into English.

The Bad Company's Direct Action Branch had only had the comm chips for a few weeks and weren't yet accustomed to them or how best to optimally employ them.

We're where you saw us last, but we're dug in better. My people are burning through their ammunition. It's like an endless tide. I'm not sure we have enough bullets to kill them all, Joseph reported.

Have you tried not shooting them?

The first bunch got close and you know Fitzroy isn't afraid to break into pugilist form. These things rammed him and bit the holy hell out of him before we could blow their stalk-heads off. He said punching them was like hitting a tree trunk. I wailed on one with my sword. I'll second his observation. It took a lot to cut through that neck. I don't recommend we devolve into hand-to-hand.

Joseph and Petricia were vampires, exceptionally strong and fast.

If you had a problem with the Tiskers, then we're fucked if we run out of ammo, Terry replied. *Where are my goddamn mechs?*

Coming, Kaeden replied. Enhanced by nanocytes, Terry and Char's adopted son was in charge of the small mech section, powered one-person armor suits. They were the tanks of the Etheric Federation. Bigger targets but they could take a beating while delivering their fair share of death and destruction.

Terry thought he could feel the ground shaking as the mechs pounded their way toward him, since they drew an inordinate amount of incoming fire.

Kae and the other three mechs of his team were on their way.

"Get down!" Terry bellowed at Christina. She was standing and blasting away at a small mob of incoming Tiskers.

"Fuck these guys!" she yelled over her shoulder, sounding too much like Terry Henry himself. She was still angry about not being able to change into her Pricolici form.

"Might as well hide inside a mech," she mumbled.

"Might as well. Now stay down!" Terry shouted. "There are snipers in the back of that mob."

Terry ran behind her position, varying his speed and zigging at odd times. He dove behind cover and crawled the last few meters to reach her. She fired one last time and bent down, keeping her eyes above a small berm so she could watch. Terry kneeled next to her and looked out.

"I know how powerful and well-trained you are. You wouldn't be out here if you weren't. But if one of these Tisker slugs hit you in the head, you'll be dead, just like any of us. I really don't want to tell your parents that I got their daughter killed."

Christina glanced toward Terry. "I've never had to sit back and wait to get attacked. It's a little frustrating."

Terry laughed out loud. "No shit! That makes you one of us. We all fucking hate this. Trench warfare sucks mongo bistok balls, if I got the expression right."

"Never heard it before, but I get your meaning. I think I'll use that." Christina leaned over the berm, fired twice, and returned to watching.

"Nice shot," Terry said as the Tisker's stalk-head turned into a blue mist from the impact of the hypervelocity dart.

Christina smiled and nodded slowly.

"Don't doubt that you're one of us, Christina. And don't doubt us. We dropped into the middle of a shitstorm. We're going to figure this out, roll up these blue fucks, and end this war. Then we're going to look at what we did wrong to put ourselves in this position. And that's on me. It's my fault that we're ass-jammed inside a circle jerk. So, stay down. Think about how bad I'd feel if you got killed?"

"How bad you'd feel?"

Terry slapped her on the shoulder. "Welcome aboard. Now kill those two so I can get going."

Christina snapped her attention back over the berm where two of the enemy were approaching quickly. "I don't know," she said before firing two rounds, "how these goofy-looking bastards—" Two more shots fired. "—can move so fast."

Terry peeked over Christina's shoulder as she continued to double-tap approaching Tiskers. "You got me. Those stumpy legs of theirs. We'll probably never know."

"Go!" Christina called as she sent a steady stream of darts into the enemy.

Terry ran, staying low, and stopped when he reached Petricia, Joseph's wife and also a vampire.

"How are you holding up?" he asked.

She looked at him oddly. "I can think of a thousand things I'd rather be doing," she replied matter-of-factly. Terry shrugged and held up one hand. There was nothing he could do about that.

Terry turned toward the enemy, gripped his Jean Dukes Special in both hands, braced himself, and stood up, angling forward as if he expected to stop a speeding train with just his body.

He aimed at the middle of the attacking mob and fired. He grunted at the force of the kick, but laughed softly when the entire mass of stalk-headed, turtle-shelled aliens exploded into a cloud of blue-mist.

"Baby's got some juice!" he exclaimed proudly.

Nice one, Dad, Kae said over the comm chip. Terry looked around and was unable to spot the mechs.

Drone, Kaeden added.

Terry looked up to see the micro-drone hovering soundlessly twenty meters over his head. He smiled and gave it the thumbs up before jumping out of the small depression that Petricia was using for cover and running for the next position.

Timmons, Sue, Shonna, Merrit, Aaron, and Yanmei were crouched in the bottom of a shell crater.

"One artillery round and you're all toast," Terry declared.

"They already shot here once. It'll be a while before they drop a second one," Timmons replied confidently.

"What in the hell kind of logic is that?" Terry asked.

"It's the best I got, boss," Timmons answered with a shrug.

Terry wanted to argue, but couldn't. They were all pinned down, and any cover was good cover. "Has anyone seen my dog?" Terry asked.

I'm not your dog, dumbass, Dokken told him.

Where are you, buddy?

Next hole. Is there anything you can do about that screaming whine? It's bugging the shit out of me.

I only hear the explosions, Terry replied before thinking about what Dokken had meant. Terry changed direction. *Kae, can your suit sensors detect sounds beyond human hearing? Dokken hears something.*

There was a brief delay. Terry prepared to run to the next position where other tactical team members were hunkered down.

Got it and triangulated. Want me to shove a rocket up their ass? Kae asked.

Terry smiled. *Make it two.*

In moments, two rockets screamed skyward and raced toward the Tisker lines. The rockets juked back and forth before diving into a rear area.

Thank you, Dokken said.

Terry bolted for the next position, zig-zagging as he ran, even though there was no incoming fire. He kept his head down and dove into the position, nearly landing on the German Shepherd.

ON BOARD the *War Axe*

"What do we do now?" Clodagh Shortall asked her department head. Commander Suresha shrugged. The engines were idling as the ship waited in the gravity neutral nexus between the seventh planet of the Tissikinnon system and its largest moon. The captain expected to hold position where they would remain undetected until Terry Henry signaled for a pickup.

"Let's focus on keeping our power signature minimized. Thrusters only to maintain position. Gravitic engines idle and the gate engines shut down," the captain replied.

The four department heads and their deputies filled the captain's small briefing room located to the side of the destroyer's bridge. One hatch led to the bridge, and the other to a corridor. The bridge was located toward the rear of the ship at nearly its highest point.

For space combat, the design wasn't optimal, but that wasn't what the *War Axe* was built for. It was uniquely suited to deliver a ground combat unit into hostile territory, because at the end of the day, the people calling the shots lived on space stations or planets.

And those were the ones that Terry Henry Walton's Direct Action Branch dealt with. The DAB, a private conflict solution enterprise, was a wholly owned subsidiary of the Bad Company.

It was Micky San Marino's job to deliver Terry and his people to the hot spots. The Bad Company signed the contracts, received half payment up front, and then inserted the teams where they decided they could most quickly accomplish the mission. Terry did the dirty work and Micky acted as a high-speed space taxi and security service.

That was the premise anyway. This was the first such effort. Micky had listened to Terry's conversation with Nathan Lowell and General Lance Reynolds. The captain wondered if every mission would be the same.

"No plan survives first contact," Micky said aloud, then clapped a hand over his mouth. Those were the last words that Terry shared before boarding his drop ship and launching from the *War Axe*.

"Tissikinnon Four," Commander Oscar Wirth, head of ship's stores, started, looking at his fellow department heads. "I get the impression that they are burning through ammunition more quickly than they anticipated. What is the resupply plan?"

Commander Blagun Lagunov, ship's structure, blew out a breath and shook his head. "We just finished fixing the ship from our last trip into orbit," he complained. "Those fighters are small, but they pack a punch. Did you ever figure out where they came from?"

Micky nodded slowly. "A small resupply station in orbit. Looks like the rest of them, little more than a ground-mapping satellite, but that's where the surviving fighters recovered."

K'Thrall rubbed his mandibles together. The Yollin's carapace was pressed against the table as he leaned forward from his chair. "I think we will purge the sky of them should they attempt another attack on the *War Axe*," he stated boldly in Yollin, which was instantly translated into the language that each member around the table best understood.

The advantages of Kurtherian nanocyte programming and the engineering marvel known as the Pod Doc. Every member of the crew as well as every warrior from the Bad Company was modified in some way by the Pod Doc.

They were all better for it. They could communicate without radios. They could understand other languages, instantly, as if raised speaking them.

"That's what you said last time!" Blagun said, contorting his face and scratching his head.

"Ballistic drop?" Suresha suggested. A high-speed pass of the planet where they would shoot an unpowered canister into a target window, and it would then guide itself toward designated coordinates.

"Possibly." Micky stroked his chin in thought. He looked at Commander MacEachthighearna, but Mac simply shook his head. As the environmental department head, he was focused exclusively on the *War Axe's* internal systems.

"Take the *War Axe* to the surface?" Suresha asked skeptically.

"Not my first choice," the captain answered candidly. The destroyer was unable to protect itself when on the ground. "You think those fighters are exo-atmospheric only?"

Suresha nodded confidently. "Those are space fighters only. I'd bet my engines on that one."

"I don't like that option at all," Commander Lagunov

said, wincing at the thought of exposing the ship to fire from above and below.

The captain looked from face to face. "Blagun. Prepare a ballistic canister, just in case. We'll pray that TH and company can accomplish their mission with their initial deployment stock."

"We can hope," Blagun replied, nodding, his lips turning white as he pressed them together. "I'll have that canister ready within eight hours."

The captain tipped his chin to the stores department head. "If there's nothing else?" he asked. No one had anything. "Break's over. Back on your heads."

Blagun shook his head, recalling the captain's favorite joke. A man dies and goes to hell. He gets put in a room where people are standing in a knee-deep cesspool smoking and joking. He looks at them and says, "This isn't so bad." That's when the demon says, "Break's over, back on your heads."

Blagun didn't think he served in hell, but sometimes, it was hellacious work, and he needed to get back to it.

2

Tissikinnon Four

Team leads, meet me at my position in three, Terry passed to the company via their internal comm chips. Forty-eight souls were counting on him to lead them successfully in battle. He wondered briefly if any of them wouldn't be going home.

With a snarl, he forced his errant thoughts down. He popped his head over the small berm, looked, and ducked back down. A bullet slammed into the berm, sending a dirt shower over him.

Kae. Did you see where that shot came from? You'd think a stalk-head with spindly arms wouldn't be a good shot, but damn!

The mech's cannon opened up, spitting thunder. The air sizzled as the railgun rounds screamed downrange. *Chew on that, you piece of shit,* Kae growled as he ran over the top of a ridge and headed toward his father.

Char, Joseph, Timmons, Marcie, and Aaron loped from five different directions. They varied their speed and zigzagged, diving into the hole one by one. Dokken ducked behind the big human to avoid getting crushed.

"Would you look at what the cat dragged in," Terry said.

The cat? Dokken said, looking past Terry's leg, expecting to see the good king Wenceslaus.

"Sorry, buddy, just an expression." Terry nodded toward the enemy lines. Kae scanned the horizon before carefully entering the hole and sitting down.

"No movement. With the death of that last sniper, they seem to have lost their desire to stick their necks out," Kae replied using the suit's external speakers.

"Stalk-heads sticking their necks out. Nice one," Terry Henry told his son. Char groaned.

"I still don't get you, TH. We're in the middle of the shit and that's where you find the most stuff to laugh at," Joseph said slowly.

"It's his way," Char answered. She smiled at her husband, her purple eyes sparkling under the muted Tissikinnon sun.

Marcie showed no emotions as she watched the others. Timmons and Aaron shook their heads, a werewolf and a weretiger, friends. Even though they'd been raised in two different societies, they were all members of Char's pack. Even Joseph, the vampire.

And Terry had conscripted all of them to be members of the Bad Company.

"Bunch of crap, huh?" Terry said with a chuckle. "I've already made a note that before we sign another contract, whoever wrote the RFP is going to get tortured until we get the straight scoop. And for the record, after we finish this, I am going to beat the shit out of that pencil-necked dweeb of a president."

"You're not going to torture anyone and you know it, but I fully support a good pummeling of the Crenellian president. That lying fuck deserves a knuckle massage of his face."

Marcie smiled and nodded. "In the meantime," she said, eyes narrowing, "we're going to beat the shit out of some Tiskers. I know that we don't want to kill them all because we don't want them vulnerable to other enemies, but I really want to send these fuckers back to the stone ages."

"I hear that," Kaeden said. He wanted to unleash his mech unit on the Tisker forces, but they still didn't know the breadth of the Tisker forces or firepower.

"We're surrounded," Terry said matter-of-factly. "We're surrounded and no matter which way we shoot, we're going to hit something. That may seem like it makes sense, but it doesn't. I want to dictate the terms of this engagement, not respond to what they're doing. So, I'd like to move us to high ground, on their flank, and start rolling them up."

Kaeden vibrated with anticipation. He wanted to be turned loose. He'd trained with the other members of his small team on board the *War Axe*, but the simulators didn't do the suits justice. There was nothing like feeling the woosh of an actual rocket launching or feeling the impact through the soles of the mech's boots, leaning into the kick of the massive railgun.

Terry slapped a hand onto the cold metal surrounding his son.

"Kae's team will create a diversion that will look like

the main attack. Stay low, hit fast, and hit hard. Keep moving." Terry used his silvered knife to draw in the dirt at the bottom of the crater. Dokken sniffed at the ad hoc map. Terry blocked him with his leg to keep the German Shepherd from peeing on the diorama.

"Marcie and Joseph. I'll need you and your people to hold that flank as we head up this ridgeline." Terry pointed at the ground with his knife and then pointed over the berm toward the high ground to their right.

"Aaron. I'll need you and your people to head up our right flank. You'll be on the military crest on the far side of that ridge, which means we won't be able to see you. I suggest you change into Were form and cover the ground at top speed."

"We can do that. Christina, too?" Aaron asked.

"Unleash the Pricolici, but you are not to engage. I want you to get into place here—" Terry stabbed his knife into the map. "—and cover our approach. Timmons. You're with us. We're taking it right up the gut, but I expect the mechs will be drawing all the fire. Questions?"

"What do we do when we get there?" Joseph asked.

"We find the flank of these bastards, and then we roll it up." Terry pondered his statement. "What are the drones seeing?"

"Blue stalk-heads for as far as the eye can see in all directions. They aren't massed in any one place, just scattered, and a metric fuck-ton of them."

"I'm going to kill that president," Terry snarled.

"I'll hold the door for you," Char told him while darting glances over the berm. Terry watched her before risking a look.

"Motherfuck!" Terry pulled his Jean Dukes Special and dialed it down to five. "Get ready to run back and prep your people. We leave as soon as we repel this blue tide. Kae, I think it's time for you and your people to unleash a little hate and discontent."

Kae spoke within his helmet to the other team members. Within ten seconds, the thunder of their footsteps echoed over the crater. With a nod to Kae, Terry leaned over the berm and fired as rapidly as he could pull the trigger.

Kae stood and unleashed his railgun across a wide arc. Terry ducked down and covered his ears after the first hundred rounds raced past his head.

The others jumped up and ran from the crater. Rounds from the other mechs joined Kaeden's. He stepped beyond the berm and then started running toward the enemy. Terry holstered his pistol and bolted after Char.

AARON LOPED across the cratered area and dodged behind a small bank where Yanmei was crouched, uncomfortably holding her railgun. She was a hand-to-hand warrior, preferring combat while in weretiger form. She maintained her disdain for weapons, even though she carried one. Aaron leaned close to be sure.

It hadn't been fired.

"Christina!" he shouted at a figure braced against a small rock, firing with nearly reckless abandon. "Conserve your ammo!"

She turned with a guilty look. He waved at her to join

him. She jumped up and fired sideways as she ran. Aaron wondered if she was hitting anything, although the more he learned about her, the more he discovered that she was a gifted warrior, trained to a level most of them couldn't imagine.

No wonder she was frustrated.

She stopped short of cover and took aim, firing methodically. "AAHHHH!" she yelled after sending ten deadly slivers at hypersonic speeds into the enemy.

"Do you believe that? Takes two shots to finish them. No matter where you hit them, you need to blast 'em again." She started to lean out from behind cover before Aaron pulled her back.

She relaxed. He held out a hand in a calming gesture.

"We'll need to change into Were form and then run as fast as we can over that way." Aaron pointed indiscriminately. Yanmei tried to see what he was trying to show them. "And then we go up there and cover the rest who will be approaching from that direction."

More non-specific waving. The two women looked at each other and shook their heads slightly. Neither had any idea where they were supposed to go.

"Jones!" Aaron shouted through cupped hands.

"Sir!" came the reply from somewhere out of sight. *Can I help you?*

"I keep forgetting about these things," Aaron complained, before putting a finger to his temple and closing his eyes.

"He really works at it, doesn't he?" Christina asked.

"You have no idea," Yanmei replied, watching her

husband's lips move as he communicated using the chip in his head.

"Okay," Aaron said, smiling as he opened his eyes. "They'll follow us up, quick as they can. Can you carry our weapons when you're, you know, a wolf?"

Christina ducked her head to look at Aaron and Yanmei from beneath her eyebrows. Her face started to change, and she grew in height. She snapped her jaws. "Yeessssss," she said, flexing her muscles and reaching out a talon-like claw.

Yanmei handed over her railgun. Christina slung it over her back. Aaron handed his to her and both the weretigers quickly undressed. They bundled their clothes into their backpacks and held them out.

Christina rolled her eyes. "Todddday, a paaaack muuuuule, but noooow, we fiiiiiiighttt," she said before throwing the packs over her back. She pointed her snout skyward and roared her joy at being in Pricolici form.

Two weretigers appeared at her side, jaws wide, showing their great fangs, as they dug their razor-sharp claws into the dirt. With a monumental leap, Aaron was off. Yanmei and Christina bolted after him. The Pricolici looked unbalanced running upright, but the strength in her legs propelled her.

Still, the great cats were faster as they flowed over the ground in their race toward the ridge. Christina stopped to adjust the gear she carried, her eyes flashing yellow in her anger at being relegated to servant.

weretiger snarls and screams galvanized her into action. She accelerated, sending clods of mud behind her as her claws ripped into the ground.

Ahead, four Tiskers and two weretigers were engaged in a melee with blue blood and tufts of fur flying through the air. The Tiskers fired repeatedly at point-blank range, but the weretigers kept moving in a deadly feline dance.

Christina forgot about the weapons strapped across her back. Her eyes glowed yellow as the Pricolici within raged to the fore. She darted through an opening and dove, her front claws digging into the neck of the blue creature.

She pushed off the shell with her back legs and spun around the creature's neck, digging deep into the stalk. With a violent jerk, she ripped through and tore off the blue head. Christina launched herself at her next target.

The Tiskers fired again and again from their hand blasters, but the weretigers were moving quickly, foiling the aim by erratic direction changes, but some rounds still hit.

Both weretigers were bleeding heavily from multiple wounds, but they hadn't slowed down. Fangs and claws struck again and again. The shells protected the creatures. Aaron and Yanmei knew that, too. They sought to get closer, rip the stalks with their claws.

Kill their enemies.

Christina was blown sideways by the force of the bullets hitting her. She twisted mid-air, rolling so when she landed, she was on all fours. She tore the ground up as she surged into her enemy.

She only saw the one before her, focused on its vulnerable neck, protected by two spindly tentacles that flowed like wheat under a summer breeze. The fire was deadly accurate when a target stood still long enough.

Christina had no intention of being that target. She hit

the Tisker's shell and jumped to the side, catching a tentacle on her claws and using that to pull herself inward. She ripped the muscles, rendering the tentacle useless as she let go. With a great overhead slash, she tore the creature's eyes from its head.

The Tisker flailed, firing haphazardly in the direction of the Pricolici. She ripped its arm off before attacking the stalk on which its head spasmed.

Aaron jumped, wrapped his front paws around the Tisker's tentacles, and pinned them to the stalk rising out the middle of the creature's shellback. He sunk his fangs into the Tisker's neck, growling and twisting as he tried to tear out his enemy's throat.

Yanmei had been more graceful, attacking in quick hits, slashing the stalk, jumping away, and diving back in. Blue blood flowed down the creature's stalk and onto its shell. Its tentacles hung slack, the weapons having already fallen from numb digits. Her target was walking dead.

She pounced one last time and slashed through the creature's head, splitting it open and spilling its blue brains over its shell. Yanmei stumbled off the shell as the Tisker's stumpy legs failed, and it dropped to the ground.

Christina staggered away, finally taking stock of the damage done to her. The healing process was already well underway. That didn't mean it didn't hurt.

Tisker bullets hurt like hell.

From nearby, the sound of four mech-sized railguns consumed the world of sound with its relentless noise.

3

Kaeden was on the point of the diamond formation, rushing forward. Praeter was to his left. Cantor was on the right, and Duncan followed in reserve, ready to exploit success or reinforce failure, whatever he was needed to do.

The railgun burped twenty rounds. Kae swept the weapon from left to right, sending short bursts of the hypervelocity rounds screaming into the enemy ranks.

Like skirmishers of old, they were scattered across the field of battle as the mechs surged quickly forward, angels of death sweeping the area clear of the blue Tiskers.

Praeter and Cantor followed suit, yelling as they unleashed the destruction that such weapons made possible.

"Easy on the ammo," Kae cautioned before turning his attention back to the enemy, which seemed to be scattered across the rolling plain in front for as far as they could see. "Eyeballs."

Immediately, two micro-drones vaulted from the back

of the mech suit and raced skyward. Kae picked the targets that were shooting at him to fire on. He kept his formation from moving in a straight line. They sped up. They slowed down.

It wasn't long before the artillery arrived, exploding where they'd been, not where they were, not where they were going to be.

One hit too close and threw Duncan on his face. The mech scrambled to get up.

"Ramming speed!" Kaeden ordered.

TERRY WAITED until the first round of incoming artillery hit. The rest of the Bad Company's Direct Action Branch was loaded and ready to move.

"Go, go, go!" he shouted the order for a tactical movement to the ridge and further up the valley until they held the high ground on what was originally their flank.

Tactical movement. Terry's euphemism for run like hell. Kimber barked an order and her platoon of FDG warriors turned mercenaries ran in squads, organized by fire teams, keeping their spacing but still looking like a mob as they raced over the broken terrain.

The Pod Doc enhancements had made them all stronger and faster. Their teamwork and attitudes had made them what they were well before they were enhanced.

With pride, Terry watched the unit he'd built back on Earth with standards from the old Marine Corps. He knew that the Marines would have been happy to see that their brand of warfare would transcend the Milky Way, and be considered the premier combat unit within the growing Federation.

At least Lance Reynolds and Nathan Lowell considered Terry's Force de Guerre that way. Terry Henry wondered if he'd been set up with the mission to Tissikinnon Four.

A rite of passage.

"I'll be damned," Terry said as he signaled the other teams to head out. Joseph and Petricia ran, staying between the four warriors and the incoming rounds. They slowed their pace so the warriors could keep up. Vampiric speed was a completely different gear. When Joseph and Petricia moved as fast as they were able, they turned into a blur.

In combat, they were deadly, but it wasn't in their nature to fight. Terry watched the two vampires protect the warriors by using their bodies as shields. He expected no less from his leadership team.

He watched Marcie, Ramses, Auburn, and Cory staying close to the platoon. Kim and Ramses provided the military leadership while Auburn and Cory were in support. Marcie was second to Terry Henry.

She was with the others, for the moment, but would promptly dart off in a different direction. She needed more information, to help the colonel best manage the battle.

Auburn didn't look happy, not because he was assigned to his wife's unit, but because he was the Direct Action Branch's logistician.

He had nothing to issue. He carried a radio that he could use to contact the ship and order supplies. That was the extent of his purpose on the ground. He carried a shotgun for close quarters combat, for defensive purposes only. He could run as fast as most of Terry and Char's inner circle, but he wasn't a fighter either.

Cory was the unit's healer. Terry and Char's natural daughter, she was born with a mutated version of her parent's combined nanocytes. She could heal injuries, coax the wounded back from the brink of death. She always stayed near her husband, Ramses, just like Terry and Char stayed close to each other.

Cory was one of the best in hand-to-hand combat, she had been raised that way, but she didn't want to fight. Many considered her to be the nicest person they'd ever met. She preferred that to taking lives. She kept the others calm with her presence and helped keep her father from embracing the rage that tickled the dark corners of his being.

Terry's family from before the fall of mankind had been murdered on the fateful day, the World's Worst Day Ever. When TH found them, he'd gone on a rampage and killed everyone who was there. To this day, he carried the knife of the gang leader. Kaeden carried the other knife that Terry had taken from the man after he'd cut his head off.

To intimidate the others.

It worked, and they ran. But Terry was a Marine and they were punks. They died tired. And Terry had gone into a self-imposed exile. It wasn't his place to eliminate all humanity for the crimes of a few. He had wanted to, so he disappeared. For twenty years, he stayed away.

He had returned one hundred and thirty-one years ago with a singular focus to help drag the people back to civilization.

Now, he was doing that on an intergalactic scale.

For money.

Terry was okay with that because he got to pick which side he fought for. And this was his test. He needed to find the head of the serpent and cut it off, save the lives of the Tisker warriors.

The werewolves Timmons, Sue, Shonna, and Merrit followed the vampires, at a distance, separated to limit their vulnerability to incoming explosive rounds. The warriors on Timmons's tactical team followed, using a similar box formation to the four Were.

Terry, Char, and Dokken were last, waiting until there was enough distance before running out.

Music started playing in the direction of the mechs. It wasn't hard to hear, even over the noise of combat.

"Is that Johnny Cash?" Terry asked.

Char nodded. "Yep. Kae discovered it in the archives. He always has music playing now. His tastes are rather extensive. The *War Axe* seems to have it all."

"How did I not know this?" Terry leaned left and right as he scanned the battlefield, ready to alter the plan if the enemy countered in an unexpected way. But the Tiskers were singularly focused on the four mechs tearing through their haphazard ranks.

"Too busy preparing for war to live the life of a Gen X-er?" Char offered.

"Is that what I'm supposed to be?" Terry replied with a chuckle. "I never thought of myself that way. I'm not the most cultured. You may have noticed."

"I may have," Char answered, shaking her head. She peered around Terry's shoulder, then checked the progress of the company. "It's time, lover."

I wondered, Dokken added, before launching himself from the small depression and flying over the open ground, pounding with all four feet. Terry and Char took off after him.

After one hundred meters, Terry spun in a circle, seeing that the Tiskers were advancing toward the positions that the Bad Company had just abandoned.

"Good enough," he said as he turned back and accelerated to catch up.

Start working your way toward the ridgeline, he ordered the mech unit using his comm chip.

Yes, sir! Kae replied happily. The mechs went from jogging to running, increasing to maximum speed. They stopped firing to save ammunition, using the power and momentum of the mech suits themselves to run over intransigent Tiskers. At full speed, the mechs bowled through the enemy forces. The tentacle-held weapons were useless against the Kurtherian-designed armor.

Kae and the others swung in an arc on a tangent away from their real goal, headed up and over a ridge in the distance. They'd swing around and approach the high ground from behind. Terry saw the dark dots of the microdrones as they weaved back and forth ahead and to the flank of the mechs.

They disappeared into the distance, just like Johnny Cash's dulcet baritone.

Char and Dokken had sped up. Terry redoubled his efforts until a cascade of dirt rained down on him from the impact of incoming artillery. He dove for cover.

AARON AND YANMEI started to run again. The artillery pounded at the back of their senses before they realized that the others were already on their way and the weretigers were supposed to have been in position. Yanmei took the lead, loping with a limp as blood trailed down the golden fur covering her back leg. Her chest fur was coated in red and blue blood.

Hers and that of her enemies.

Aaron trotted after her, weaving as he ran. Christina had been shot too, repeatedly, but the Tiskers hadn't hit anything vital. "Damn, sluuuug throooowersssssssss," she grumbled as she ran past the injured weretigers. Their wounds were healing, but not as quickly as the Pricolici's. She ran a hand down each of their sides, letting them know as she ran ahead. They both rubbed their heads on the Pricolici's thigh, letting her know that they were okay.

She still carried their weapons and backpacks, despite the gymnastics of her attacks.

Christina ran ahead, staying on the military crest as Terry had directed. Running on the top of a hill skylined the individual. Staying near the top, but below head level, they used the hill to block the line of sight. Although there were Tiskers far to the right of them, the bulk of the blue forces to their left couldn't see the Weres.

For the win, Christina thought as she continued toward the target ahead. Two Tiskers ambled out of nowhere, slow, but quickly in how they managed to get in the way.

She slid a railgun from around her and stabbed a claw through the trigger housing. She pulled back. "Wellll-cooome to myyyyyy nighttttt marrrrrre," she panted as the

31

railgun sent a stream of hypervelocity needles through the two blue bodies.

The Pricolici chuckled as the weretigers caught up with her. She waved an arm and started to run toward their goal. It wasn't much farther ahead. The impact and explosions of artillery sounded far off. She wondered how long it would take the others to reach the hilltop.

MARCIE SURGED AHEAD of the others, racing along the side of the shallow ridge. Her eyes scanned side to side, up and down as she looked for an enemy.

She found none. Smiling darkly, she slowed to let the others reach her. Over one shoulder, she saw the Pricolici and the weretigers loping toward the goal. They'd all reach it at the same time.

It was the first time she'd seen Christina in her Were form. Terrifying. Walking upright, back slightly hunched, fangs prominent in a canine muzzle and claws, unlike those of werewolves, more like the weretigers. Pricolici— with the deadliest features of all the Were.

And she carried a railgun with a claw on the trigger.

Terrifying. It was the only way to describe her. Marcie committed to spending more time with her, befriend her. Stay away from her *bad* side.

Ramses, Auburn, and Cory arrived next. They'd passed Kimber and her platoon when they realized that no one was shooting at them. They took advantage of the opening to run faster in a straight line.

Cory waved to Christina, signaling that she wanted to

look at Christina's injuries, along with those of the weretigers.

"Oooookkkaaaaay," Christina managed and tipped her chin toward Aaron and Yanmei. Cory didn't argue. The Pricolici looked past her to the battlefield beyond as she stood guard over the others.

Both Aaron and Yanmei changed back into human form. Two backpacks landed with a thud beside them. Christina waved a claw at them. Aaron groaned as he reached for it, then stopped and smiled.

"I remember," he said. For more than a century, Aaron had been plagued by the fact that he never remembered what happened when he was in Were form. After Yanmei joined him, she would have to tell him what he did. He suspected she left out the grizzly details to spare him from being afraid to change.

But now he could remember his recent time as a weretiger.

All of them, every single one of the FDG who boarded the *War Axe,* had spent time in the Pod Doc, getting nanocytes if they had none, and tweaks if they did. Aaron's nanos had been fixed.

He looked at the wounds on his chest, but shrugged them off. Cory put her hands on her hips and looked them over. She was limited in how many people she could help in a day. The nanocytes would flow from her into the injury. It exhausted her to share them, but her body would put her to sleep before she lost too many.

Sometimes that happened when it was most inopportune. Ramses stayed close by, to carry her to safety should she pass out. He kept one eye on her and one eye on the platoon running up the last incline. Kimber was already directing them to establish a perimeter, start digging in.

"We'll be fine, Cory," Aaron told her as he and Yanmei started to get dressed.

"What happened back there?" Cory asked, still concerned.

"Some Tiskers showed up and they aren't as easy to kill as we would like," Aaron stated simply.

"Uh huh," she replied, frowning. She turned away from the weretigers and sat next to Ramses. He watched the platoon settle into position, while keeping a wary eye out for the rest of the company.

"It's quiet," Cory said.

"Sometimes the silence is the hardest thing to hear," Ramses added. "The diversion has run its course, I suspect."

Ramses kneeled and put his hand to the ground where he could feel the rhythmic thumping of mechs running toward them. "Can you feel it?"

Cory nodded.

The landscape was mostly barren, short growing stumps barely passing for trees. There was no grass, only spiky weeds. It was an inhospitable environment except for one thing: it was oxygen-rich.

The humans embraced the boost to their metabolisms. It also made for bigger explosions.

There was no warning besides the final whistle of the approaching shell. The lightning reactions of a well-trained force drove them all prone before the explosion.

All but one. Christina was picked up and thrown as if carried on the wings of a tornado.

4

Terry shook his head, his ears still ringing from the nearby explosion.

"Char!" he yelled and started scrabbling through the rocks, pulling himself in the direction he'd last seen her.

Here, she said using the comm chip. Terry stopped and turned his head back and forth.

"Where?" he asked.

"Right here," she said from a short way ahead. "I need a little help."

Terry jumped up and ran the few steps to get to Charumati before ducking back down after a number of snap-fired rounds ricocheted from the rocks around him. Char was seated, but buried up to her chest in debris. Terry pulled the rocks and threw them down the gently sloping hill behind him.

More rounds impacted the dirt and rocks. Terry pulled faster, digging with his hands until he could pull the purple-eyed werewolf free. She couldn't stand because both her legs were broken. He lifted her up and started to run.

"Wait!" she cried. "Dokken was underneath me."

Terry gently put her on the ground. A slug slammed into his chest and a second one tore through the meat of his upper thigh. "We're sitting ducks out here. Order covering fire!"

Char closed her eyes to concentrate on sending the message.

Terry started digging again until he found a dog's paw. Terry stepped into the hole and carefully removed debris until he could pull the German Shepherd free. The dog was unconscious, but breathing. Terry held Dokken in his arms, looked at Char, and put Dokken back down. He pulled his Jean Dukes Special, took aim, and braced himself as he dialed it to ten.

In a rapid sequence, he sent the rounds across the battlefield behind him, firing at anything that hinted at blue. Terry thought he might have taken a shot at the sky in his rush to stop the incoming fire. After forty-seven shots, his shoulder started to ache. He put the pistol away and reached for Dokken.

The dog started to stir, his eyelids fluttering as he came to. *The fuck?*

"Damn, buddy. I thought you were more cultured than to swear like that."

The human I seem to have adopted is a bad influence. I seem unable to walk at present. May I impose upon you for a ride? Dokken asked.

Terry clenched his jaw and nodded. He picked the dog

up and cradled him to his chest as he left the hole and joined Char.

"I see," she said, still sitting on the ground. The hammering of the earth told them that at least one mech was coming. Terry handed Dokken to Char, and then bent low to pick up her and the dog.

He grunted as he worked his way upright.

"By all that's holy, TH, you'd think I weighed a ton!"

Terry smiled down at her. "I think I'm just getting weak in my old age."

Dokken laid his head on Char's chest and closed his eyes.

Kae and Cantor pounded up to them. Kae stopped and Cantor continued a few steps down the hill, raised his rail-gun, aimed, and fired a shot every few seconds.

"One shot, one kill," Cantor said through his suit's speakers. Kaeden leaned down to relieve his father of his burden, but Terry shook his head.

"Cover us," he ordered, and he started hiking uphill.

Kae walked backward, staying between the enemy and his parents. He fired occasionally, but the Tiskers appeared to be tired of this fight and were leaving the humans to their own.

Maybe the Tiskers were tired of dying. The battlefield, which the Bad Company had been dropped in the middle of, carried a blue sheen from the amount of blood spilled.

"I wonder how many stalk-heads died today?" Kaeden asked.

"A lot more than should have, and someone is going to answer for that," Terry promised.

Unnamed Corner of the Pan Galaxy

"I'm not sure you understand my position, Mister President," Nathan explained, trying to remain calm.

"I paid for service. Give me service!" the small humanoid alien raged.

"The fight appears to be different than you led us to believe. Such a material change of condition alters the contract," Nathan said slowly, enunciating each word.

The president interrupted him.

"Shut up!" Nathan added, the muscles in his cheeks flexing as he fought to keep from yelling. "When Colonel Walton cleans up that mess on Tissikinnon Four, I'm sending him and his people to you, so you can see the people you tried to send to their deaths. I pray for your sake that you're more convincing with him than you've been with me. You had best start practicing your lies now to improve your delivery. Then again, an acceptable alternative may be to pay whatever Terry Henry Walton tells you to pay after the mission is accomplished.

"However, he may prefer to take payment out of your hide. He already said he was going to burn your palace to the ground, so you've got that to look forward to." Nathan touched the screen to sign off before the weasel-faced president could reply.

Nathan rubbed his temples before pulling a Pepsi from his refrigerator. He rolled the cool can back and forth over his forehead. Nathan hadn't told the president that his daughter was down there, with Terry Henry, in the middle of another man's war.

He knew that she was well-trained and enhanced to a

high level, but he still worried. A couple slugs to the head could ruin anyone's day.

Maybe he would send Terry to renegotiate payment once the Direct Action Branch ended the Tissikinnon Four war.

If there even was a war. Nathan couldn't be sure of anything, and Terry was overdue with his latest report. He drummed his fingers on the table.

Nothing to do but wait.

TISSIKINNON FOUR – FIREBASE GLORIA

"Christina? Christina!" Cory shouted.

After the explosion, Christina had unconsciously changed back to human form. Blood streamed down her face and from her ears. Cory held Christina by her shoulders and gently shook her.

Cory put her hands on Christina's neck and massaged gently. "What happened?" she asked.

"Hilltop go boom," Cory replied as the woman's pupils danced in her head.

"Very funny," Christina mumbled, closing her eyes and trying to relax to let her body heal itself.

"Where the fuck did that thing come from?" Marcie growled. Praeter and Duncan had launched their micro-drones and were scanning the enemy lines. "Well?"

"Nothing yet, ma'am. Their pieces must be *way* in the rear," Praeter reported. Artillery pieces. Something that the Bad Company had been told didn't exist.

"They have some serious hardware out there. How come we can't see it?" Marcie wondered.

No one had an answer. Most were still working through the ringing in their ears from the near-miss that almost took the top off their hill. At least it had created a crater that they could use for cover if need be.

"NICE JOB, KIMBER," Terry told his daughter. "It's too bad we won't be able to stay for long."

She twisted her mouth as she nodded. "Remember the Maginot Line? A monument to man's inability to adapt to modern warfare."

"I have no idea what you're talking about."

Char chuckled as she stood gingerly on her newly healed legs. Dokken was curled up by her feet. Terry looked at them both, before making eye contact with Cory. He tipped his chin toward the dog. She hurried to the big German Shepherd and kneeled by his side.

Cory's eyes glowed blue. They had for over a hundred years, ever since she healed the vampire Akio. He carried special nanocytes, as did she. The two mixed and blended, giving her the ability to light up the night, even when she didn't mean to.

She carried sunglasses to cover her eyes at night when they couldn't be seen. In the middle of the day? It didn't matter. Like now. Her eyes were a beacon that radiated calm to all who were near.

Like Dokken. He relaxed under her touch.

"Broken ribs," Cory said as she ran her hands over his sides. "Scrapes and cuts." The blue of her nanocytes appeared beneath her hands as she healed the worst of

Dokken's injuries. When she finished, her head sagged and shoulders hunched.

Ramses kneeled next to her and draped an arm around her shoulders. She took a deep breath and together, they stood. Dokken opened his eyes, and took in his surroundings before getting his paws underneath himself and pushing upright. He wagged his tail and dog-smiled. He stood on his back legs and put his front paws over Cory's shoulder as if the two were preparing to dance.

With one massive lick, he splattered Cory's face from chin to forehead. She tried to move away, but he had her. He moved in for a second lick.

She dodged back and forth, until Ramses stepped in and gently pushed Dokken down. He ruffled the dog's ears.

I like you. I got stuck with that one, Dokken told Cordelia, pointing with his eyes toward Terry Henry Walton.

Cory leaned down to eye-level. *I need you to take care of him. He will do anything for us and usually that means sticking his neck out. I need you to keep him safe. It'll be our secret.*

Char stood next to Terry. While he surveyed the battlefield and raced through a series of tactics to implement to achieve mission success, Char watched her daughter and the German Shepherd. Cory had made another friend.

They said that she never met a stranger, because they all became her friends.

"This is a shit show," Terry lamented.

Dokken appeared at his side and leaned against him.

"Hey, boy! I'm glad you're all right," Terry said without

looking down. He dropped his hand to Dokken's head and scratched behind his ears. "Team leaders, up!"

Kae hurried up, still in his mech suit, and took a knee so he wouldn't tower over the others. Joseph and Petricia both moved in. Marcie, Auburn, and Kimber stood to the side. Timmons, Sue, Aaron, and Yanmei rounded out the leadership team. Terry waved for them to follow him.

Christina joined the group. Terry nodded his approval.

He moved to a small depression on the side of the ridge where they weren't so exposed.

"We need to start over," he said without preamble. "We now know that everything we were told is wrong. Our mission was supposed to be simple. Remove the Tisker leadership. We were to land behind their lines and take care of business. Without the military leadership, the premise was that the soldiers would be spared and peace would be restored.

"Hotheads. We were to knock off a few upstarts hiding behind an army. As it was, the landing coordinates were boned. We get dropped off right in the middle of the army with no idea where that supposed leadership might be. Has anyone seen any Crenellian forces? Small humanoids, look like that cheesedick president?"

Everyone shook their head.

"We need to find those fuckers, too. So. We need to pause our combat operations and collect intel. Since there's nothing like hearing it from the horse's mouth, Timmons, I need you to take your team and Christina and capture a Tisker. He? She? Needs to be healthy. Capture it without hurting it, if you can. Kaeden. I need your unit's drones expanding a three-hundred-and-sixty-degree perimeter.

Go as far as you can and find me something that looks like a headquarters. If not that, then let's find the heavy artillery. The *War Axe* can drop a few surprises when they come by with a resupply. Auburn. Can you handle setting that up?"

"No problem," he replied. "When and where?"

"As soon as possible. We burned through a week's worth of ammo in a few hours. We've gained nothing, and we're already seeing empty magazines."

"We've gained something," Marcie offered. "We gave them one hell of a bloody nose."

"They're using old-fashioned slug-throwers, and we have railguns," Terry said, not trying to dampen Marcie's spirits, but to keep things in perspective. "I admire their courage, but they're going to change tactics soon, and I think it's going to be raining artillery. Not just a few rounds here and there, but it's going to level this area. We're going to get blown apart, and we're all going to die if we don't keep moving. Auburn, set up a resupply drop in the valley between the two ridges about ten clicks to the north-northeast.

"Kimber, I need you to move your platoon near the resupply point and set up a long skirmish line to protect that valley. Move out as soon as it's dark. We'll stay here and keep them occupied. Aaron, take your people and move ahead of the platoon. Show them the way."

"If my math is correct, that leaves us with you, Char…" Terry hesitated as he pointed at the remaining faces and tapped the air in front of his face. "That's about sixteen of us to make it look like all of us."

"Don't forget the mechs."

"Indeed." Terry pursed his lips and looked at Petricia's still unfired railgun. "That'll work."

"Let's get to it. Build me an intel picture of what we're up against. I hate killing front line guys. They're just following orders, so let's find the ones giving the orders, and then we'll introduce ourselves." Terry patted his Jean Dukes Special.

Colonel Terry Henry Walton carried the pistol that could end wars.

ON BOARD the *War Axe*

Auburn's image filled the screen. Commander Oscar Wirth and Captain San Marino watched as the Bad Company's logistician detailed the supplies that were needed.

Oscar checked items off the pad he carried. The canister was already filled with most of what Auburn ordered, but there was an issue.

"I can send you the mechs or I can send you ammunition. I can't send both," Oscar explained.

"Terry's not going to be happy," Auburn replied, "but I think he'll understand. And then we need a second canister prepared, just in case."

"That's the problem. We don't have a second can. But I'll order the construction of a second and third as soon as we sign off. It will take a few days before the next can is ready and a few days after that for the third one."

"We're going to be down here with our asses hanging out," Auburn said, looked off-screen, grabbed the camera, and the image blurred. A muffled explosion sounded from nearby. "Hang on."

After two more explosions, Auburn held the camera away from his face as he lay sideways on the ground. "Getting a little hot here, so I figure we'll be moving soon. When do you think you can make the drop?"

Oscar looked to the captain. Micky looked at the ceiling for a moment before answering. "Thirty-two hours."

Auburn whistled. "I better let you go. Earlier would be better. I'll tell Terry the bad news."

The screen went blank. Oscar felt like crap. The captain slapped him on the shoulder. "Go do your thing, Commander," Micky told his department head. "I need to get this ship moving."

5

Tissikinnon Four

The darkness was nearly absolute. The moons orbiting the planet were small and reflected very little light. Four was at the far edge of the Goldilocks Zone and received less light and warmth because of it. Three was at the closest edge of the zone, but had never developed life. The aliens from Four had established a settlement there with the help of their spacefaring neighbors, the Crenellians.

The current conflict came about because the Crenellians expected access to Tissikinnon Four for mining operations as payment for their role in helping the Tiskers into space. The Tiskers had balked at their part of the deal, even though from what Terry had seen, the Crenellians weren't going to strip mine the planet, only dig underground and reclaim the area as they finished.

"How in the hell did they negotiate a contract like that?" Terry wondered.

"I suspect a lot of show & tell, pointing and grunting,

with the Crenellians simply writing down what they wanted and the Tiskers accepted, having no idea what they agreed to because they received weapons!" Char sneered.

Terry had chosen the project because he didn't like people making a deal and then backing out when it came time to fulfill their part of the bargain. He wondered if the contract that he'd seen was real. Everything else seemed to be a lie. He gritted his teeth.

"What if the Tiskers are the ones we should be fighting for?" Terry asked. Char rubbed his shoulders. They were tight, not from combat or lack of sleep, but from carrying the burden of the entire Federation, to fight for the innocent and bring them justice.

"There's all kinds of wrong going on here. I think when we get to the bottom of it, we'll find that these two systems deserve each other," Char suggested.

Terry looked into the darkness. Even with his enhanced vision, it was tough to see anything. He could barely see the warriors from Joseph's tactical team, and they were less than ten meters away.

The darkness made the distant flashes stand out. "Drop a rocket on their ass!" Terry shouted to the mech unit. "TAKE COVER!"

The warriors planted their faces in the dirt and covered their heads, hoping they didn't get their asses blown off.

Four rockets screamed into the night, milliseconds before they heard the whistle of the incoming rounds. The shells shattered the night's calm in an instant, reshaping the landscape around them from barren to cratered and torn.

When the short barrage ended, Terry lifted his head.

Char was safe by his side. The darkness had returned. Explosions in the distance signaled the arrival of Kaeden's rockets. The secondary explosions said they hit their target. More explosions racked the enemy unit followed by a fire that burned out of control.

"REPORT!" Terry ordered as he stood, pulling Char to her feet before dusting himself off.

He heard the others checking with their people.

Miraculously, no one was injured. Marcie picked her way carefully across the broken ground.

"They know where we are," Marcie stated the obvious. "Time to move?"

"I think so. Rally the troops and get on your way. You take point, and Char and I will hold down tail end Charlie." Terry paced as he thought, hands clasped behind his back. He carried his pack with his Mameluke sword behind it and his pistol. He had left his whip on the *War Axe.*

He had carried the whip for a long time, but figured it was due to be retired. He wanted to put it on display in his office. The weapon that he and Char had used to help them defeat Marcus, the greatest of the werewolves.

A Jean Dukes Special. Micro-drones. weretigers. Mechs. A Pricolici. Railguns. werewolves and vampires. Rockets and swords.

Terry ran through the inventory of the arsenal that they brought to the planet surface. None if it mattered if he didn't know where to aim. He had an incomparable fighting force at his command, and he would get them all killed if they ran out of ammunition, ran out of places to run.

He needed the intel, and for that, he needed the

patience to wait for his people to do as he had asked, bring back those bits and pieces of information that he could use to paint a picture from which he could determine their next steps.

I'm hungry, Dokken said, bringing Terry back to the present.

"Here you go, buddy." Terry reached into his combat vest and pulled a big chunk of beef jerky. "I've heard bistok tastes like bacon."

If all you ever have is bistok, anything different is good, the dog replied.

"Words of wisdom, right there. If every day were Christmas, it wouldn't be Christmas."

Dokken looked up at Terry. He smiled at the German Shepherd. "We need to get the fuck out of here," Terry said.

My thoughts exactly, human, Dokken replied.

"Mine too, dog."

TIMMONS LOOKED at his hostage capture team—Sue, Shonna, Merrit, and Christina. "Sue and I will stay in human form, while I think we need our werewolves to guide us through the darkness, use the Etheric to find a lone enemy, and bring him in."

Christina relished the opportunity to change into her Pricolici form. She was pleased with her decision to join Terry Henry Walton's expedition to the far reaches of the Federation. Exporting justice, they'd said. Sounded good at the time. Sounded even better when she was turned loose on an unsuspecting enemy.

Timmons could see the look on her face. She was happy. He'd seen the same look on only two other people as they prepared to go into battle. Terry Henry and Marcie. They were at home in the chaos and horror of combat, preferring it over the drudgery of day-to-day life.

Sometimes it scared him, but as he thought more about it, he was relieved that such people existed, and that he was on the same side. People like that fought because they wanted to, taking the burden from those who fought because they had to.

Timmons would do as he needed to do. For the pack.

For his alpha.

"Let's get us a fucking Tisker," he growled. He tapped the shortsword he carried. "If it gives us any grief, we hack off its tentacles. As long as it can talk, it'll be useful. If we have to kill it? Then we kill it and go find another one. I don't want to dick around out here any longer than we have to."

Shonna and Merrit stripped off their clothes, put them in their backpacks, and stuffed them into a hole in the ground. They changed into werewolves, Shonna, shaggy gray, and Merrit, a dark brown. Christina wore loose clothing that stretched. She didn't need to get naked in front of the others.

She saw how nonchalant they were about it, as well as indifferent. Christina liked their attitudes. *I can be friends with these people. They remind me of the good people I had the honor to know as I grew up,* she thought.

Christina changed into her Pricolici form and stretched, enjoying the power of her Were body. Timmons watched her. "We need them alive," he told her, looking intentionally at her claws.

"Offf courssssssse," she replied, looking down at the werewolf.

"Of course." He laughed. Shonna and Merrit stood on all fours, fangs bared. "Can you feel them?"

Shonna and Merrit nodded. The Etheric dimension allowed them to see outside of reality, but also living things that affected the dimension, like those drawing power from it. Shonna and Merrit saw the entirety of the Bad Company, figures in the mists, the closer ones clearer than those farther away.

The power they drew was clear, too. Terry and Char drew more than most of the others. The warriors drew less as their nanocyte programming wasn't as complex.

The Tiskers were faint shadows against the fog. Shonna, Merrit, and Christina bolted into the darkness.

"Dammit!" Timmons swore under his breath as he and Sue raced after the others. He could barely make out where he was stepping.

He peeked into the Etheric and saw a pair of Tiskers not far away. The werewolves were angling in one direction while the Pricolici was circling to come at the enemy from the other side.

Timmons and Sue were running straight at them. Someone had to determine which Tisker would live and which would die. That someone was Timmons, and he had four seconds to decide.

"WHAT DO YOU SEE?" Terry asked Char as they followed the others into a wide valley between the hills.

"Aaron and Yanmei far ahead, moving deliberately. The platoon is close together, maybe too close."

"I'm making a list of how badly I fucked this up," he whispered through gritted teeth. "You'd think I never fought a battle before."

"Not like this you haven't, and not with anything like this at your command, lover," Char whispered back.

Terry chewed on her words before digging at himself. "Night vision, infrared, better intel, confirmation of landing coordinates *before* we land, and an objective that I can touch. Next time, we'll meet personally with whoever submits the RFP. I can't have this again."

"None of us can have this again, but you'll always be you. You'll hold an after-action review following the battle and incorporate those into the Bad Company's direct-action standard operating procedures. Your SOP will always be under construction," Char replied in her most reassuring whisper. "I have to agree that this was a shit sandwich served by ass monkeys during a goat rope."

Terry looked at his wife. Even in the darkness, her eyes sparkled with purple glints. The silver streak of hair trailed down one side of her face, the only hint of her werewolf nature. "I don't deserve you," he said softly.

"I know, but after one hundred and thirty years of putting up with your shit, you've grown on me."

"After the first century, it's all downhill," Terry whispered as he ran his hand down her arm. They gripped each other's hands for a moment before turning their attention back to their tactical movement to a secondary position that they would occupy for as long as they could before heading toward where the resupply canister would land.

Char kept one of her two nine-millimeter pistols in hand. She had a railgun slung over one shoulder, but her pistols had become a part of her, having carried them almost as long as she'd known TH. Prizes taken from one of mankind's enemies.

Terry had been carrying an M1911A1 .45 caliber pistol, but after firing the Jean Dukes Special, he carried that and his sword.

"If I'm in the thick of things, wailing away on an alien, then no one is driving the boat. I need to stay out of the battle as much as possible, let the others fight," he had told her.

And Terry Henry Walton had been right. Char watched him look into the night, not seeing anything in the darkness as his mind wargamed battle after battle in order to find a course of action that would give him the result he desired. Maximum victory with minimum casualties.

On board the *War Axe*

"The second ballistic canister won't be ready in time," Commander Wirth stated over the comm system. Captain San Marino looked at the screen, but didn't let his disappointment show.

"Then we'll deliver one canister now and the second one as soon as it is ready."

"I'll let you know when it's going to be ready," the commander said before signing off.

Micky San Marino looked back to the screens that

replicated windows looking from the bridge into space. The ship had been under constant acceleration for two hours. To those on Tissikinnon Four, they wouldn't even register as a speck of light in the night sky.

It would take another six hours before becoming a pinpoint and another twelve hours before those on the planet would recognize that the speck of light was moving.

"Targeting the fighter buoy?" Micky asked.

"Yes, sir," helm replied. "Twenty-six hours to impact."

"Weapons control. Where are we on the analysis of their last attack?"

K'thrall spun in his chair as he closed his holo screens. "Smedley and I have analyzed their attacks. They use their small size, speed, and agility to their advantage. We believe that by bringing the defensive arrays to full strength, firing before we arrive, we will deny areas of space in which they can maneuver. We channel them into kill zones where our main weaponry fires shorter range but broader bursts," the Yollin explained.

Micky held one finger in front of his lips as he thought about the scenario.

"If we conduct preemptive fire, won't we be vulnerable if they penetrate our defenses or come in from behind us?"

"For a few milliseconds, yes, as we change over from pre-targeted space to auto-tracking."

"Ammunition burn?"

"Won't be an issue," K'Thrall replied. "At the speed we'll be traveling, we'll remain in the engagement envelope for less than ten seconds."

"That could be a long ten seconds," Micky intoned slowly.

"For reference, our last pass over Tissikinnon Four exposed the *War Axe* for more than two minutes."

"If they review that engagement like we just did, what are they going to see as our vulnerabilities?"

"That's a good question," K'Thrall said. "Smedley, can you put yourself in their place and tell us what you think?"

"Of course. Standby," Smedley said, using expressions that he'd been picking up from Terry Henry Walton.

The imitation wasn't lost on the captain. TH didn't demand respect. He earned it. Even from the EI.

"The lack of maneuverability is the greatest weakness shown. Last time the space fighters attacked, they hit the *War Axe* everywhere but forward. In addition to doing more of that, they could place mines in our path for a passive attack in addition to high-speed strikes from pre-positioned spacecraft."

"Can we see the fighters?"

"Not if they are stationary and in a low-power mode. At the speed we'll be closing, our active systems will not be able to differentiate them from space junk before we are well past," Smedley explained patiently, his wise, old voice coming through the bridge's overhead sound system.

"If they are in low power mode, will they be able to catch us when we pass?" Micky asked.

"By my calculations, they will not. They could fire from a static position."

"What I'm hearing is that we need to be maneuverable and not come in on a predictable flight path." The captain climbed down from his chair on a platform overlooking the bridge crew. He strolled casually to his helm officer.

"Can you do that, Clifton?"

The man spun around to look at the captain. His face was contorted as he tried to fight against the sarcasm on the tip of his tongue. "Did you have something in mind?" he asked instead of making a smartass comment.

"We don't need to adjust very far. Five kilometers, maybe ten at the last second. A massive thruster burn on one side of the ship, jolt us out of a predicted flight path. If they have ships prepositioned or mines in our path, that little bit should be enough to ruin their plans."

Clifton nodded slowly. "Yes. I can do that. We'll be heading toward one side of the fighter buoy and then jump to the other to take it out. We hit the atmosphere and use friction to slow us down while we dump the canister, then accelerate on a slingshot around the planet and head back for deep space."

"Sounds like you already had it figured out," Micky told the man. "Make it so. And, K'Thrall, make sure we don't run out of ammunition in the ten seconds we're in their attack envelope. Smedley, if you come up with anything else, let me know soonest. We'll be committed pretty soon and won't be able to adjust after that."

Tissikinnon Four – the dark of night

Marcie moved forward between the units. She was by herself, but using her ability to see into the Etheric to maintain her awareness. Besides the Bad Company, the Tiskers appeared to have retreated, abandoning the valley.

The weretigers at the front continued to move more slowly than they were capable of, and Marcie wasn't sure why. Her senses told her that it was clear.

Trust the weretigers, she thought. When they stopped and spread apart, she started to run. The platoon halted and hit the deck at the sound of a person running.

"Colonel Walton, coming through!" she cried as she continued to run. The platoon was wary, even though Tiskers made little sound when moving and didn't speak English.

She accelerated past the platoon. "What's going on?" Kimber asked as Marcie passed.

"The weretigers sense something," she replied.

"How do you know?" Kimber wondered, sure that Marcie hadn't heard her. "Platoon, inverted V formation, NOW!"

Marcie was almost on top of the weretigers when the Tiskers appeared. Two, then four, then eight. A weretiger scream split the night. Marcie aimed and fired as fast as she could pull the trigger.

"Weapons tight!" Kimber shouted as the platoon rushed forward. They could see nothing in the darkness, and there were three friendlies up ahead. Kimber yelled ahead, hoping that Marcie heard her over the roar of her railgun. "Marcie! Where do you want us?"

6

The sound of the great cat's scream came a second before a single railgun's firing echoed across the valley. Terry ran two steps forward and stopped.

This battle would be fought without him.

"Joseph, right flank!" Terry yelled in the direction he expected the vampire to be.

"Heading out now," came Joseph's measured reply. Terry heard the orders issued. Joseph and Petricia's eyes were better than Terry's or Char's in the darkness.

Kaeden. I know you're still flying your drones, but I think we walked into something and could use your mechs, Terry said using the comm chip to communicate with his son.

Recalling the micro-drones. Heading your way now, Kaeden reported efficiently.

Once the recall was issued for the drones, they would return to the mech and reattach themselves without further direction. Kae and his team were free to engage.

Terry and Char hurried wide to cover the left flank.

When they looked back, Cory's glowing eyes were clear, showing where she and Ramses were.

"Put on your sunglasses!" Terry said softly.

The glow disappeared and everything became inky black once again.

———

"PICK UP THE PACE, GENTLEMEN," Kaeden ordered using the suit's communication system. With their infrared heads-up display engaged, they could see as if running through the twilight. The Tiskers burned half as brightly as any of the humans, with the Were registering brightest of all.

Kae saw his wife in the distance, at least, he expected that was Marcie firing and moving like a demon within a growing group of Tiskers. He counted fifteen.

Moments later, it was twenty. Marcie fired and moved, and fired again. The weretigers were nearby, darting in and out as they avoided combat, knowing that they couldn't stand paw-to-claw with the Tiskers in the darkness. The enemy seemed able to coordinate and operate without a negative impact, but then again, this was their home planet.

Where are they coming from, Marcie? Kae asked using the comm chip as the four mechs pounded across the open ground.

Fuck if I know, she replied tersely. The railgun continued to bark, spewing hypervelocity rounds at the cyclic rate. The barrel of her rifle looked hot as lava on the infrared.

A red light flashed in the lower corner of Kaeden's

HUD. Power was getting low. When it stopped flashing, he'd be out of commission until it could get recharged by the sun or an external power source. They hadn't brought one of those because of the weight and the long days followed by a short night.

They hadn't expected the extreme operations tempo. It was less than halfway through the night and he was almost out of juice.

We're coming, Marcie, Kae told his wife.

TIMMONS DIDN'T HESITATE. As soon as he saw the first Tisker, he fired, raking it from its shell up the stalk that led to its head. Sue fired from beside him, but only two shots.

"Converge and capture!" Timmons yelled as he ran toward the remaining enemy. A slug hit him in the chest, nearly knocking him over, but his ballistic vest stopped it. Sue dove sideways.

"Converge and capture?" she mumbled as she hit the ground, then jumped back to her feet when she heard the impact of three furry bodies simultaneously slamming into the Tisker. A snarl and snapping jaws.

Timmons and Sue ran into the fray and found two of the Tisker's four tentacles torn off and flopping on the ground. Christina was standing on the creature's shellback, one claw wrapped around the stalk and a second claw shaking the slug-thrower free from one of its two remaining tentacles.

The gray werewolf's jaws were clamped tightly on the

other tentacle, while Merrit darted in to take a bite from one of the creature's stumpy legs.

"Leave it!" Timmons ordered, prodding Merrit with his foot. The werewolf turned and snapped, before relaxing. All of a sudden, the Tisker stopped fighting.

Sue immediately looked into the Etheric to see if reinforcements were coming. "Nothing nearby," she reported.

Timmons pulled the rope that he'd placed on top of the gear in his pack and wrapped it around the Tisker's stalk while Christina held the creature's neck steady, keeping it from biting Timmons.

"Dooo theeeey biiiiite?" she asked?

Timmons hesitated for a moment, before tying the Tisker's tentacles to its stalk. "I don't know. If it does, we'll find out how many times I can punch it in its ugly stalk-head before it dies. Then we'll have to find another one."

A railgun opened up in the distant valley. As they started to drag the Tisker, the mechs pounded in that direction, the same direction they were going.

"We have company," Sue said, firing into the darkness.

JOSEPH KNEW there was nothing on the right flank. The ridge provided a commanding view, but wasn't close enough that Joseph could occupy it. With Petricia and his four warriors, he ordered them to run. He was determined to flank the Tiskers up ahead.

He could sense the platoon to his left as he passed. They were in an attack formation but holding steady as they waited for a clear target ahead.

Marcie was in the middle of a growing mass of Tiskers. The weretigers lunged and circled outside the enemy, but hesitated to engage.

"Hurry up!" Joseph encouraged the others. He sped ahead and angled toward the enemy. He started to fire, using his superior night vision to pick the blue shells of the enemy. Their stalks and head moved sinuously and faded with the darkness.

Petricia caught up with him and started to fire. She swept her railgun from one point to another, not firing at the center of the mass where Marcie was fighting for her life. Joseph fired and fired, using short bursts to clear a path. He ran through the enemy, using their mob tactics against them.

He lost sight of Petricia but her railgun continued to send hypervelocity darts into the Tiskers.

Marcie screamed in fury as she fired, slowly, railgun in one hand and a combat kukri knife in the other. She fired, slashed, hacked, and fired again. Joseph jumped into the circle with her.

They stood back to back and he fired outward. Petricia burst through and joined them. The three together fought furiously against the crush of the enemy. They surged inward, only to be driven back until Marcie's railgun finally clicked empty. She backed between Joseph and Petricia as she let the rifle flip behind her, hanging from its combat sling. She switched her knife to her right hand and crouched. Ready to attack again.

The rest of Joseph's team arrived and fired only when they were on top of the enemy.

"HERE!" Joseph roared over the relentless cracks of the

railguns.

The ground shook as the mechs approached. With too many friendlies, they didn't fire. They waded into the mass of bodies and hammered them with punches from their metal fists.

Jones broke through and took his place between Marcie and the enemy. The other three humans and two weretigers jumped into the circle, expanding it as they gained the edge before a new flood of Tiskers threatened to envelope them.

"There's a tunnel," Kaeden reported using the suit's external speakers. "FIRE IN THE HOLE!"

Joseph, Petricia, Jones, and the others collapsed into the center of the circle and covered their ears as the explosion shook the ground. The Tiskers stopped and then started scrambling away. The railguns opened up.

The mechs fired their heavy guns at the retreating enemy.

"CEASE FIRE!" Terry Henry Walton bellowed from nearby. Silence returned along with abject darkness. "Report."

Marcie slapped Joseph on the shoulder and nodded. "Marcie here," she said softly, knowing that Terry had exceptional hearing. Her ears were ringing from the incessant railgun fire, but that would clear up soon. "They appeared out of nowhere. Aaron and Yanmei sensed them before they showed up, and I want to know how."

They waited until the weretigers changed back into human form.

Kae showed up and hugged his wife. Terry looked around, confused.

"It's out of power," Kae reported. "Cantor is finished, too. But Praeter and Duncan have enough left to hopefully get us to morning, protect the suits until they recharge enough for us to head out."

Kae and Marcie both understood. The Bad Company couldn't stay there. Movement was their key to survival. Marcie took her ballistic vest off. It was peppered with Tisker slugs and useless to stop more. The creases in her helmet said that she was lucky to be alive. She held up her railgun.

"Spot me a few rounds?" she asked.

"Sure, Colonel," Terry said. He held out his hand and Char slapped a heavy dart pack into it. He passed it to Marcie, who swapped the empty pack for the full one and did a quick function check. She sighed audibly.

"They travel underground," Terry said.

"Looks like it," Kae answered. Aaron and Yanmei appeared, still naked, but torn up. They had been in Were form without body armor.

As if by magic, Cory and Ramses appeared, and she immediately started working on the two weretigers.

"How did you know they were coming?" Terry asked.

"We could feel them moving under the ground. The air that they pushed in front of them smelled foul. It came up before they did."

Terry nodded. "Good to know, you two. Now get yourselves healed up. Marcie, take the company up the ridge and dig in."

Marcie nodded and with one last look at Kaeden, she headed toward the platoon to find Kimber.

"Thanks for getting in the middle of that, saving

Marcie," Kae told Joseph and Petricia. He shook hands with each before he turned and disappeared into the night.

"You seem to be the best suited to work in this soup, so if you would be so kind and scout out the ridge, I'd appreciate it. I can't see my hand in front of my face. Talk about seeing, has anyone seen my dog?"

How many times do I have to tell you that I'm not your dog? Dokken replied.

"Damn, boy! Where have you been?"

Those thundersticks of yours hurt my ears, so I went the other way, Dokken explained.

"Can you see in this?"

Probably as poorly as you, but I'm a dog. I can smell my way as well as keep three feet on the ground at all times.

"Makes sense." Terry leaned down so he could scratch behind Dokken's ears. "Can you feel them underground? Smell the air they push in front of them?"

I think so. I know what to look for thanks to the cats, Dokken replied.

It was easy to see where Cory was. Terry followed the blue glow until he found her, Aaron, and Yanmei.

Ramses was coordinating with Kimber to police the Tisker slug-throwers from the ambush site. Most of the platoon members carried at least two. Some had five, but seeing how quickly they were burning through their supply of ammunition, they wanted the slug-throwers for backup.

Cory stood up weakly. Terry and Char each grabbed an arm to support their daughter. "They'll be fine," she mumbled before passing out. Terry caught her and lifted her, cradling her like a baby.

"As light as ever," Terry said, watching her sleep. Char brushed the hair from her face. "Dokken. Lead the way, buddy. Take us up the hill so we can settle in for the rest of what I hope is an uneventful night."

TIMMONS JOINED Sue in her rapid-fire response to a Tisker incursion. Four of them appeared out of nowhere. The werewolves snarled, staying close to the prisoner, while Christina was torn between staying where she was on the Tisker's shell or killing it and diving into the fray.

But the attack was soon over as all four Tiskers lay in their own blood. Sue and Timmons checked the area and found that it was clear once again.

"Come on, you blue piece of shit," Timmons growled, yanking on the rope.

"Why don't you stay as you are," Timmons told Christina. "And you two change back. Grab your railguns. werewolves are ineffective against these blue fuckers."

They dragged their recalcitrant captive back to the hole where the backpacks were stashed. They waited while Shonna and Merrit got dressed.

Timmons held the rope while Sue aimed her rifle at the alien's stalk-head. Christina rode on the shell with a clawed hand wrapped around the stalk, ready to rip should the situation arise.

But the Tisker remained sedate. It never showed the pain it had to be in with two of its four tentacles having been violently ripped from its body.

"Maybe you don't feel pain like we do," Timmons

pondered. "You have to feel something. We'll find what that is and leverage it to get what we want to know. I almost feel sorry for you. Almost. You make me feel like I'm walking a pet pig, now COME ALONG!"

Sue clicked her tongue at her mate for yelling into the darkness while in enemy territory. The five of them and one Tisker. They wouldn't be able to hold off a concerted attack.

"Would they kill one of their own to get us?" Timmons asked in a hushed tone as he yanked on the rope yet again to keep the prisoner moving.

"We've seen that they are plenty willing to die for their cause. I haven't seen any blue-on-blue fire, but I wouldn't put it past them," Sue answered in a whisper, grabbing the rope to help Timmons drag the Tisker.

Christina continued to balance on the alien's shell, tapping her claws at various points along its stalk in search of a place where it might feel pain. She wasn't sure that she was being very encouraging, but she was ready to kill it if they were attacked again.

The Pricolici refused to sacrifice one of the others to accomplish their mission of capturing one of the enemy. They could always find another Tisker. She would not be able to find another pack. Not like this one. She was feeling more and more at home with every passing minute. They needed her and she needed them.

"Yessssss," she cooed to the back of the Tisker's stalk-head. The others kept moving toward where they'd heard the firefight. Silence, darkness, and a prisoner with all the energy of a sandbag kept them from moving quickly.

7

Kaeden and Cantor crouched next to their powerless mech suits. The two men carried railguns with full loads of ammunition. The two functioning mechs stood vigil, quietly embracing their low-power mode.

Kae wanted to listen to music, to help offset his rising anxiety.

The power he felt while inside the mech was equaled by how helpless he felt without it. He'd been in combat a hundred times as a foot soldier, an FDG warrior, but the powered, armored suit changed his entire perspective on warfare. It made him feel naked as he crouched outside of it, waiting for daylight.

Kimber approached as the platoon finished their sweep of the area.

"You need anything?" she asked.

"Power," he replied forlornly.

"Need an extra fire team?"

"No. Once we juice up, we'll need to move and quickly. I don't want to leave anyone with their ass hanging out."

"See you at the top," Kimber told him, before pulling him up and into a hug. "Don't die trying to protect a hunk of metal."

Kae didn't reply as he'd been thinking about exactly that. Not dying, but protecting his suit with every fiber of his being until he could put it back on and power its weapons. Then, there would be hell to pay.

Could he leave it behind? He wasn't sure he could, so he nodded and bit his lip instead of lying to his sister.

She faded into the night, issuing orders to the platoon as she went. With low-voiced replies, the platoon moved out. The vampires had already broken the trail.

The weretigers were taking it easy, moving with the platoon until they recovered from the beating they took from Tisker slug-throwers.

The werewolves were off somewhere trying to capture a Tisker. That left Kae's parents. Terry and Char waited until the others were well up the hill before they said their good-byes and left, only to stop and head the other way. Without a word, they walked into the valley that had taken the company time and effort to cross.

Kae and Cantor sat side by side, one on each side of Kae's mech.

"Where are they going?" Cantor asked.

"We don't have to guess." Kae switched to his comm chip. *Where are you guys going?*

Timmons is inbound and it looks like they have a Tisker with them, Terry replied.

"Now we wait," Kae said.

"This fucking sucks," Cantor replied.

"I'm not sure you have that right. The question is, how can we make this suck more?" Kae joked.

In the distance, flashes looked like lightning.

"That's how," Cantor said.

"INCOMING!" Kaeden yelled toward his parents, before dodging around the backside of his idle armor.

———

"You HAVE GOT to be shitting me," Terry growled as Char grabbed his hand and pulled him sideways. He stumbled into a depression, and they both threw themselves against the side facing the incoming fire. They crouched and covered their heads, waiting for the telltale whistle of the artillery round just before it impacted.

———

TIMMONS HEARD KAEDEN'S WARNING. They had their backs to the horizon and hadn't seen the flashes.

"Get down," Timmons ordered. Everyone dropped where they were except for the Tisker and Christina. She slid around the stalk, putting it between her and the artillery pieces.

The first round impacted at the edge of the valley ahead of them, at the base of the hill, where the company had engaged in a firefight.

"I don't expect our people are still there. I think the

Tiskers have yet to learn that the best place to be isn't where you were," Timmons repeated what he'd heard Terry Henry say on more than one occasion. TH was a fan of being a moving target. He didn't like digging in. His only concept of defense was offense. Attack the enemy until they gave up or were dead.

Timmons continued, "This must really grate on Terry's soul—not having a target to hit. We run around in the open while they take pot-shots at us. It's like being on the wrong end of a shooting gallery. This isn't one of our better operations."

TERRY AND CHAR heard Timmons's order to get down. They weren't more than fifty yards away.

The first round impacted near the blown-up tunnel mouth. The area was littered with Tisker bodies and the first impact sent blue spray in a massive arc over the area. Kae and Cantor stayed low to the ground, trusting that the suit's armor would protect them.

More rounds followed into the small area where Marcie and the vampires had unleashed death upon the Tisker incursion.

Then the firing stopped. Less than ten rounds, all impacting the same area.

KAE AND CANTOR brushed themselves off. Their night

vision was ruined until the nanocytes could help the two men recover.

"What was that about?" Cantor asked.

"Could they have called in a fire mission and it took that long, over an hour, before it was executed? That's pretty fucked up," Kae replied.

"The colonel would have our asses if we dicked around for an hour before helping someone who was neck-deep in the enemy. Can you imagine?"

"No way in hell. It also makes me feel bad. The Tiskers are dedicated, but they aren't in our league. We've already killed thousands of them. It's like shooting fish in a barrel, and it ain't right."

Cantor had no reply. The Tiskers had a standing army, so they weren't opposed to fighting, but the humans brought one massive dose of pain, to be liberally delivered.

Dad, they fired on the position where the battle took place. Accurate fire, but a day late and a dollar short. It's like we're fighting school kids.

Timmons is bringing a Tisker captive. As soon as we can talk with it, we'll find out what the hell is going on. When you have power, get the drones in the air. Our entire effort is to find the Crenellian Forces, grab them by the stacking swivel, and give them a good shake until the truth falls out. I'm not a fan of killing the Tiskers. Let's see how many we can save as we go forward. Keep your head down, son. It's my job to fix this, Terry replied.

Will do. Take care of Mom. Kae looked at his teammate. "We dig in and wait. We'll be fine since Praeter and Duncan are watching our flank."

The two men pulled their collapsible shovels and got to work.

"TIMMONS," Char said in a normal voice.

"Coming," the werewolf replied. Timmons and his team appeared at the edge of what Terry and Char could see—four people carrying railguns and a Pricolici riding on the shell of a captured Tisker.

Terry nodded approvingly. "Your boy appears to be missing a couple limbs."

Christina's canine snout bounced as she laughed in her gravelly Pricolici voice.

"He didn't need them since he still had a couple more to stuff food into his pie hole." Timmons hesitated. "Do we know how they eat?"

"All that and more on the next episode of, *What's On Your Mind, You Blue Martian!*" Terry said as he eyed the Tisker closely. "Come on down, Christina. We'll take it from here."

The Pricolici jumped. Christina changed shape mid-air and landed as a human. She twisted her head one way and then the other to loosen her neck. She pulled her weapon from her back, hefting it easily as she took her place as part of the detail surrounding the captive Tisker.

Terry gave her the thumbs up as he continued to study the prisoner. "I can't wait to hear what Joseph sees in your mind," Terry told him. The Tisker's eyes focused on Terry Henry Walton.

The head at the top of the stalk was almond-shaped

with four eyes at intervals around the stalk, front, rear, and each side. The mouth was the top of the stalk and faced the sky. The point of the almond would open occasionally as the alien took a breath.

"Where's your brain?" Terry asked. The Tisker didn't answer.

"Probably in there somewhere protected, unlike us humans with our shit out in the open for everyone to take a shot at," Char said softly as she pointed to the alien's shell.

Dokken barked once at the alien, showing his fangs and snapping his jaws, then he moved to Christina's side where he wagged his tail furiously while greeting his friend.

"It's been quiet for a good ten minutes now. That's making me nervous," Terry said, looking toward the horizon, expecting to see artillery flashes. He leaned down and felt the ground with the flat of his hand. Tissikinnon Four was calm.

The captive's stalk-head dipped toward Terry. Shonna and Merrit aimed their railguns, fingers on the triggers and ready to fire.

Terry held up his hand, signaling them to stand down. "You know that we understand, don't you? You move underground. You live underground and that's why we can't find your headquarters or the Crenellians. Everything is underground. We've only been scratching the surface, so to speak."

The Tisker leaned its head back and continued to watch Terry. The colonel put his hand on the alien's shell. "I'm sorry that we killed so many of your people" Terry didn't expound.

He knew that he'd kill more if he had to. Many more.

CANTOR SHOOK KAEDEN. "INCOMING," he told him. The flashes from the horizon were still fresh before his eyes, but when Kaeden blinked awake, he didn't see anything. Darkness enveloped with the night.

The grayish clouds blocked what little light would have come from the stars.

Kaeden ducked back into his hole. "How long till daylight?" he asked.

"I hope not long."

The first round impacted on the far side of the valley. The second hit behind them. The explosions walked up one slope and down the other. The fire seemed haphazard, random even.

"What do you think that's all about?" Cantor asked.

"We haven't seen any stalk-heads lately, so they're firing blind. That's what I think. We know they can hit what they're aiming at." Kae stopped as a round hit nearby and sprayed dirt and gravel over the two men.

Kaeden shook the dirt off and continued as if nothing had happened. "I believe they don't have eyes on target, otherwise, we'd get hammered. If they destroyed the mechs, we'd be in a world of hurt."

Cantor raised his head enough peek out of his hole. Then he stood up. "Looks like that's it for now." He brushed himself off before moving to his suit and checking it for damage. Kae did the same thing. He caressed the metal as he looked.

He'd grown extremely fond of his powered, armored suit.

TERRY AND CHAR hunched behind the Tisker. The alien stood tall and proud. With eyes on each side of its stalk-head, it didn't need to turn around to look at them. Terry found it slightly disconcerting.

"He doesn't care if he dies," Terry said matter-of-factly.

"Not in the least, but he's come this far, so it'd be a shame to lose him now," Char replied.

Joseph, where are you? Terry asked. It was a few moments before he received a reply.

Toward the top of the hill, on the back side, Joseph answered.

How far from the valley? More artillery rounds impacted through the area. Terry tried to make sense of the targeting, but it seemed like a random barrage.

It ended and the quiet returned.

"I wonder how Kurtz and the boys are doing," Terry said, standing up and helping Char to her feet. The eyes of the Tisker watched them closely.

"What made you think of them?" Char wondered.

"Kurtz always had a different view of the world, and I like him."

"I like him too, and the others. They worked hard to keep up, not an easy task. I hope their transition to becoming Were is going well. We did what we could to school them on their new abilities," Char replied.

"We left them behind to establish the FDG, build an

official special force for the Federation. I would have loved to do that." Terry stroked his chin and started walking across the valley on his way toward the rest of the company.

"You don't get to do everything. Remember the thousands of talks we've had about control?" Char asked, although it wasn't a question. She was making her point, again, like driving bamboo shoots under his fingernails. "You are doing exactly what your Empress asked you to do. The FDG is a side gig, important, of course, but General Reynolds will make sure it stays on track. We work for Nathan Lowell now. You want to control that, but I'm looking at Tissikinnon Four right now, wondering how much you have under control here?"

Terry clenched his jaw tightly as the anger rose within. Of course Char was right. She'd been right the entire time they'd been married. Terry held a fist over his head, the signal to stop moving.

He turned toward Char, his expression softening as he looked into her eyes. "Why do you put up with me?"

"What? And give up all this?" She waved her arms expansively.

Darkness weighed on them like a heavy blanket. At the edge of what Terry could see were Timmons and Sue, pulling a blue, stalk-headed alien with a rope. A large German Shepherd stood in front of them, wondering why the entourage had stopped. His lip quivered, and he showed one fang as he looked at the Tisker.

"I love you more today than yesterday, but not as much as I'll love you tomorrow." Terry leaned forward and kissed her, slowly and passionately.

"For fuck's sake!" Timmons said, exasperated. "You'd think the blue fucks weren't shooting at us or that we could see where we're going or that we knew what the fuck we were doing here."

Terry pulled back, smiling. "Jealous?"

"You got me, TH. You know that the top of my list of things to do in the middle of a shitstorm is suck your face."

Terry and Char chuckled as they faced Timmons and Sue. Sue couldn't look at them as she bit her lip to keep from laughing.

Terry locked eyes with the Tisker. "You're right, Timmons. This fellow here is going to help us find the Crenellian headquarters as well as the Tisker leadership, and we're going to set things straight, because you're all right. This is a total shit show, and I have had enough. We haven't lost anyone and I want to keep it that way."

Hungry, Dokken said. Terry patted his pockets and held his hand up. Char pulled a piece of jerky and handed it over. Timmons rolled his eyes, earning a hard slap in the shoulder from his mate.

Dokken chewed happily as he followed the trail the others had left behind.

8

Kimber crouched as she ran, reducing her silhouette, just in case the enemy was watching. From one fighting position to the next, she checked on her people. They were operating at a fifty percent stand-to, which meant one person watched while the second slept.

Dawn cast long shadows across the terrain laid out in front of the ridge they'd occupied the night before. Most of the platoon was positioned on that side. Less than a squad were dug in on the back side of the ridge. No one was on the top.

Tops of hills made for juicy artillery targets.

Marcie sat in the open and watched the lightening horizon. When Kim made it to her, she stopped and sat down.

"Do you feel anything?" Kim asked.

"No one besides us," Marcie replied, turning tired eyes toward her sister-in-law. "The others are coming up the hill now, and I think they have a Tisker with them."

Marcie had been born with nanocytes that were activated and modified following a number of significant emotional events during her time with the FDG. She'd gained the ability to see into the Etheric, something the Were or the vampires could do, but not the other nano-enhanced humans.

"I wonder how Gene would fit in here." Marcie hung her head toward her knees and closed her eyes. Kim couldn't tell if she was sad or just tired.

"I miss Gene, and the kids, and Earth," Kim said as she stood. She rested her hand gently on Marcie's head. "I don't think it will be long before Kae can power his suit up and join us."

Marcie lifted her head, slightly refreshed after pulling power from the Etheric. "I think shortly, yes." Marcie stood, nodded to Kimber, and set out to meet Terry and the group climbing the ridgeline.

ABOARD THE *WAR AXE*

"Acceleration holding steady. Speed increasing according to projections. Drive systems nominal," Clifton reported from his position at helm. He'd just returned to the watch, taking helm control back from Smedley.

He looked at the captain. Micky San Marino had been there when he left just a few hours earlier and he was still there. Clifton expected that the captain hadn't rested. He hesitated to say anything.

"Systems. Are weapons programmed and ready?" Micky asked K'Thrall.

"Not yet. The programming is extremely complex and will change as we get closer to the planet. I'm coordinating with helm control. The movements must be pre-programmed to coordinate so we don't fly into our own fire," the Yollin explained.

"Smedley? Project our timeline and trajectory on the main screen."

The Tissikinnon system appeared on the screen showing a line from where they were arcing toward the fourth planet. Time hacks showed how long it would take to the next waypoint. The captain climbed down from his chair and walked to the front of the bridge.

"Zoom in on time hack fourteen," Micky requested. "Now show me the fighter station. That's the buoy right there?"

Micky pointed.

"Yes," Smedley replied. "The buoy will be at that location, but I cannot guarantee the fighters will be there when we arrive. I assume that they will not be there."

"The plan is set for the fighters that will be somewhere in this envelope of space." K'Thrall used a small laser pointer to paint a dot on the front screen and then he drew a misshapen oval. "We base that on how far they traveled from their buoy during our last engagement."

The laser pointer disappeared and Smedley replaced the rough line with a digital cloud that showed a three-dimensional distance from the buoy.

"That's a pretty big margin of error," Mickey said softly as he walked back and forth, looking at the map from one angle and then another. "Show me the fire plan."

The screen zoomed in quickly. The *War Axe* figured prominently and a slow-motion sequence of events played out. The ship started firing at the eleven second point with a countdown. Each second took fifteen seconds to churn through as labels popped up to show each aspect of the engagement.

The ship's defensive weaponry sent out slivers of light in the direction of the buoy, maintaining a maximum sustained volume of fire for the first five seconds. After that, intermittent fire filled gaps in the cloud of projectiles.

"We're varying the railgun speeds to force the fighters away from the engagement envelope. Our plan isn't designed to kill the fighters, only to keep them from firing on us," K'Thrall explained.

"If TH does his job, then the fighters will stand down when we come back for pickup."

"We'll collect as much data as possible, just in case we need to make another resupply run before Colonel Walton can end the war."

Micky closed his eyes and groaned. "What kind of unrealistic expectations does he have to work under? The man has been given one week to end a war that's been going on for who knows how long. He takes fifty people to the planet surface and expects to take care of it. Auburn sounded surprised that they needed more ammunition, food, and water."

No one had an answer. "It's what he signed up for," the captain said, as if repeating someone else's argument. "It's what Nathan thought the Bad Company was capable of doing."

"Can they?" Clifton asked.

"I hope so. If they can't, it won't be because we didn't resupply them. K'Thrall! If a fighter comes anywhere near us, I want it blown to hell," the captain snarled. "And we'll come back as often as we need to. I want those ships to run when they see us coming. And, Oscar, I want those ballistic cannisters ready to go. I don't care what you have to do, you get that second canister ready for delivery. We're going to give them four more mechs and a power supply."

A NONDESCRIPT RIDGE on Tissikinnon Four

Terry and Joseph stood close to each other, both eyeing the captured Tisker. "Do you think the translation chip will help when you read its mind?" Terry asked.

"How would I know?" Joseph replied, unsure of how to access the alien's mind and hesitant to try.

"How would I know what you don't know?" Terry responded.

"I don't know that," Joseph answered.

Char palm-slapped her forehead. "What am I watching?"

Terry pointed to himself and tried to look innocent. "Don't you know?"

"I swear, TH, you are a real piece of work," Joseph said softly, shaking his head and holding out his hand. The two friends shook.

"Nothing like a little combat, some life and death situations to strengthen the humor muscle, toughen the funny bone, sharpen the razor wit." Terry gave the thumbs up to their blue captive. "Be cool, buddy."

TH walked away to check on the rest of the unit. Char and Dokken joined him.

Timmons, Sue, Shonna, Merrit, Christina, and Petricia stood in a loose circle around the Tisker. All eyes were on

Joseph. He held out both hands, fingers splayed, one eye closed.

"What are you doing?" Petricia asked her husband.

"I thought everyone was expecting a show. I'm just trying to deliver to my adoring fans," Joseph replied.

"Terry is rubbing off on you." Petricia put her hands on her hips, and Joseph understood the cue.

"Fine." The gifted vampire blocked the others, so their thoughts wouldn't intrude as he reached out, looking for the alien's mind. He found it, and as he expected, the thoughts were strange.

Smells and vibrations, monochromatic images, a language of tones in a range outside what humans could hear. Joseph heard the rhythmic thumping within the alien's mind, but it didn't mean anything to him. He knew the beat was language, but he didn't understand.

The bottom of the shell acted like a bass drum. Through that membrane, they sensed vibrations and made sounds of their own.

The low frequency traveled more easily through the ground, where they spent most of their lives. Joseph could see it all. Tiskers by the millions, living in vast caverns deep underground.

Tunnels to the surface. Tunnels parallel. Tunnels everywhere. And the natives. Joseph could see the vibrations, but he couldn't hear the words. He concentrated harder until he felt hands holding him, keeping him from falling.

A dark cavern with an endless fall, but something held him back from the edge.

"They are the Pod, the people of Poddern, this planet," Joseph gasped.

From far away he thought he heard familiar voices telling him to stop, but he couldn't. The conversation had only just begun.

KAEDEN HELD his breath and thumbed the power to "On."

The suit came to life and started running through its self-diagnostics. "We are back, boys and girls. Coming to you live from Budokan!" Kae said using the suit's external speakers to project his joy. The suit completed the diagnostics and then buttoned up, encasing its precious human cargo in a symbiotic relationship between man and machine.

Which prompted Kaeden to play *Rage Against the Machine* as the four mechs spread out, moving slowly as the systems charged under the early morning sun.

At twenty-five percent charge, they started to run, jogging easily across the valley and up the hill.

Killing in the Name blared as the mechs maintained an inverted V formation.

On our way, Dad, Kae reported using the comm chip in his head.

You guys are hard to miss, Terry replied proudly. *Take stations on both ends of the ridge as well as both sides. Get your drones in the air and build me a tactical picture of our position.*

HIDDEN in a remote corner of the Pan Galaxy, Nathan Lowell sat in his private office looking at the video communication screen. The President of the Bad Company frowned.

"Better than last time, Nathan, only because we've moved to the high ground. They have some artillery, but they use it oddly. The real news is that we're making progress with a captured Podder. They call this place Poddern, for reference. Joseph continues his probe of the alien's mind."

Terry looked calm and collected. He turned off-screen, left and then right, before giving Nathan his attention.

"We expect a ballistic canister dropped in about six hours. We'll be able to reload and refuel. Then we'll take it to them, assuming our Podder can give us an idea which way to go," Terry reported.

"I didn't think you took any vehicles with you," Nathan said, confused.

"Chow, Nathan. We're going to get some extra chow. We didn't expect this kind of op tempo," Terry explained. "Did you get in touch with weasel dick?"

Nathan rubbed his temples. "I expect you mean the Crenellian president. Yes, we did. I was going to make a personal visit, but the president agreed to pay the full fee now and a comparable amount when the mission is completed."

"We're getting double pay for this?" Terry requested clarification.

"Better than that. Double-time and a half, TH." Nathan leaned back. "Now tell me this is going to be worth it."

"I'd love to tell you that, Nathan, but it would be a lie. I don't know at this point. All I know is that we are slowly building a better intelligence picture. As soon as I have better fidelity on the future of this conflict, I'll let you know."

Terry ducked as an explosion shook the video. Terry stood up and gave the finger to someone or something. Railgun fire followed.

"CEASE FIRE!" Terry bellowed. One railgun barked in the silence. "I said stop firing! Timmons and Aaron, go grab those two before they get away."

"Taking more prisoners, TH?" Nathan asked.

Terry furled his brow and looked down. He took off his helmet and ran one hand through his short hair. "We have these guys so outclassed, I feel bad shooting them. We've already killed thousands of them, Nathan, and we don't have a single casualty, well, not one who hasn't healed already."

"That's a sobering number." Nathan grimaced. When he came up with the concept of the Bad Company's Direct Action Branch, he intended it to end wars and keep the dictators and despots from becoming too powerful.

The Crenellians had an agreement with the Tiskers, the Podders, that is, and the natives of Tissikinnon Four broke the contract and killed a large group of civilian workers. Nathan was starting to think that the Podders weren't in the wrong.

"Do what you need to do, Colonel Walton. I trust you, implicitly, explicitly, tacitly, and all the lees there are. I know the solution you come to will be the best for all parties. For the win, TH, and double-time and a half. Lowell out."

9

The *War Axe*

"We are on our final initial trajectory, at terminal velocity. Engines are idle," helm reported.

"Countdown to maneuver, Smedley," the captain requested. A digital timer appeared in the upper corner of the main screen.

Two minutes and forty seconds.

Micky's fingers danced across the keypad on the arm of his captain's chair. "Two and a half minutes to enemy contact," he reported on the ship-wide broadcast. "All hands, man your battle stations. Pre-position damage control parties. Seal sectional bulkheads and prepare for combat. Two minutes twenty seconds on my mark. Mark."

"No data on enemy space fighters or other ships in this region," K'Thrall reported.

No data, Micky pondered. *That means we don't know. Flying blind because of our speed. We're in front of our sensors.*

"Engines, standing by for braking maneuver,"

Commander Suresha reported over the comm system.

"Damage control bots and personnel are pre-staged and active," Commander Lagunov reported.

"Systems are nominal. Damage control bots and personnel are pre-staged and active," Commander Mac reported.

"Ballistic canister is ready for launch. Powered armor is attached to the external surface. I'm not sure how that's going to work, but it's the only thing I could come up with. Sorry, Captain," Commander Wirth said.

"It's genius, Oscar. It'll be fine," Micky replied.

"One minute, forty-five seconds," Smedley shared. The captain's eyes watched the timer counting down in the upper right corner. At this point, he was hanging on for the ride. If they needed to radically alter course, they were doomed.

"We are committed to this course of action. It is the right course and with it, we shall accomplish our objective," the captain quoted one of the Empire's old battle manuals. In space combat, second guessing oneself usually led to bad things happening, so the combat fleet trained extensively in choosing the right course early in the process.

No one stopped on a dime in space. Spaceships did not turn quickly. Most combat was done from a single pass, as the *War Axe* was about to do. Except they outflew their radars and were blind.

"One minute." Smedley sounded calm. The EI wouldn't rattle. The bridge was tense. The *War Axe* and her crew did not have extensive combat experience. The ship was relatively untested.

The seconds seemed to crawl by. The captain busied himself by checking status screens, including video feeds of various areas within the ship. Most people already had their hoods on and were strapped to their workstations.

"Thirty seconds."

Micky tapped his console. "Hoods," he ordered for all personnel in the ship. He pulled his over his head and sealed it in place. Within seconds, the console showed green.

Micky ran a finger along the outside of his console. He looked at the main screen and watched the numbers tick down.

"Twenty seconds."

"For the Bad Company. Long live the *War Axe*," Micky said.

"Systems powered. Ready to engage. Counting down," K'Thrall intoned. "Enemy fighters located. All are attached to the buoy."

"HOLD FIRE!" Micky ordered at the twelfth second.

K'Thrall's hand slashed through one of the holo projections surrounding him.

The ship jerked and the crew was slammed to one side of their seats as the pre-programmed maneuver diverted the *War Axe* five kilometers off trajectory.

The ship was heading straight for the buoy.

"May God have mercy on your souls," Micky said before the ship's forward fire control engaged to obliterate the obstruction before the ship.

The War Axe coasted through the remains of the buoy and the fighters that had been attached to it. The ship had taken no incoming fire.

Micky's heart leapt into his throat. He wasn't a big fan of fighting an enemy that didn't fight back.

The automatic fire control kicked in again.

"What are they firing at?" Micky asked quickly.

"Multiple objects dead ahead!" K'Thrall yelled. Neither of them had time to issue the next command.

Brace for impact.

PODDERN

"What the hell are you doing down there?" Terry yelled as the two tac teams continued to fight the Podders.

With a deep growl, a Pricolici appeared, vaulted over the people closest to the alien, and landed on its shell. It reacted with lightning speed and pumped shells rapidly into the Were's chest. Christina staggered backward as four tentacles, each armed with a slug-thrower, weaved and dodged as they continued to fire unerringly.

Marcie opened up with her railgun, splitting the stalk from shell to mouth. The Podder staggered and settled to the ground as its stalk and four tentacles flopped over. Timmons and his crew rushed to help the weretigers and humans each dodging defensively around the alien, refusing to give it a stationary target.

Shonna and Merrit bolted behind the creature, but it had eyes on all sides of its head. Podders couldn't be surprised.

"Stop!" Joseph called out. "Everyone just STOP!"

Joseph inched forward until he was close to the Podder. He tapped the butt of his short cavalry sword on the ground, beating a rhythm.

He stopped and waited with his eyes closed. Then he pounded again.

"Tell him to drop his weapons," Terry ordered.

Joseph held up one hand, rapped the ground again, and then waited.

"I'm not fucking around here. He needs to drop his weapons," Terry reiterated more urgently. He looked from Christina to the Podder, back to Christina. She was bleeding heavily as two warriors dragged her to a nearby fighting hole where Cory waited to help her.

"Neither am I, TH. Trust me when I say that we want to talk with this one. As long as he's not shooting anyone, does he need to drop his weapons?" Joseph asked.

"Yes, as a sign of trust."

Joseph tapped, waited, tapped again, and then stood up straight. "He asks you to drop your weapons, as a sign of trust."

"I believe my initial assessment that the Podders had only a rudimentary intelligence may have been in error," Terry admitted. He looked from person to person, Were to Were, and back to Joseph. "Everyone put your weapons down. Everyone but me. You can tell him that everyone's safety is my responsibility."

Terry moved in front of Joseph to stand before the blue alien. The eyes on its stalk-head followed him. The Jean Dukes Special hung at his side, barrel angled slightly upward. Terry could fire a killing shot within milliseconds, if he needed to.

It was dialed to five, sufficient to blow the Podder into next week.

If he needed to.

The others put their weapons down. The blue alien dropped his tentacles until the slug-throwers rested on his turtle-like shell.

"You said I wanted to talk with this one, so here we go, Joseph. I want to know two things. Where is the Crenellian headquarters, and then where is the Podder headquarters?"

Joseph dropped to a knee and tapped the ground. Terry looked over his shoulder to watch the vampire do his thing.

Several minutes passed before Joseph stood up. "He doesn't know."

"All of that and the answer is, he doesn't know?" Terry kept his eyes on the Podder. The color rose in his cheeks. He was getting angry. Char was too far away to calm him down, but Joseph could see the heat building.

"He said a lot, but understand that they don't know directions in a way that we would understand. Maybe he does know but I couldn't understand. They live their lives underground. Despite how many we see up here, the real number is in the Pod."

Terry holstered his pistol and held up his hands to the Podder.

"Thank you, but what do we really know? I need intel, my friend. I need something that will show me a way to end this war," Terry pleaded.

"Learned a bunch of stuff there, too. The Pod screwed them. The contract was signed and everyone was on board, and then they decided they didn't want to comply, so they started a rockslide and buried the Crenellians. They killed all of them. It was a massacre."

Terry squinted as he looked at Joseph. "They did what?"

"They did it, TH. They started this war." Joseph nodded toward the Podder.

"And I'm back to thinking they are barely above a rudimentary intelligence. Where does that leave us?"

Joseph shrugged. "At least we know that feeling sorry for the Podders isn't right. They brought this on themselves. And worse than that, they know it. That's why they're not trying to kill us."

"What do you mean they're not trying to kill? We've had the shit kicked out of us!" Terry's eyes shot to Christina, who was sitting up, her wounds healed. She was back in human form. Her uniform was ruined because of the abuse it had taken.

Char stood nearby. Terry couldn't read anything in her expression. Timmons and Sue held hands as they walked away. Shonna and Merrit joined them. Petricia stood behind Joseph and rested her hand lightly on his shoulder.

"Can he lead us to his people so we can talk with them more? And from there, we can hunt down the Crenellians," Terry said.

"I think he will take us underground, if we give him some reassurances, but the Crenellians, they are a different matter in entirety. As you've already guessed, they are fighting this battle by Podder rules. They're down below, and they're out for revenge."

"We're fighting a war where there are no good guys," Terry said in a low voice. "I'm pretty sure that this could not suck more. Here's what we're going to do. We're going to whip out the big hammer and beat both sides into submission, show them the real cost of war. Vengeance won't bring the Crenellians back. I'm thinking a healthy show of force will do the trick. With a precise application of max firepower, I hope both sides will be sufficiently respectful so I can tell them what they are going to do."

"Terry Henry, arbitrator to the stars," Joseph said.

"I think it's more like a divorce lawyer. You spend a lot of money and in the end, no one is happy."

"We better hurry. The Pod is putting together an army to cleanse the planet of both us and the Crenellians."

Forward fire control kept its volume of fire for the time it took to cover the distance—less than one second. The automated system wasn't able to destroy all of the objects ahead of the ship.

The explosions said they were manmade, intentionally deposited in space.

Mines.

Forward fire control was replaced by the close-in-weapon system. The cloud of energy and projectiles produced a massive fireball in front of the ship. The *War Axe's* speed sent it through the cloud as the explosions were still happening. The ship's armor and shields protected it from the millions of fragments hitting it at velocities approaching ten thousand kilometers per second.

The *War Axe* jerked violently. Metal screeched and the ship was through the field. The ship shook with vibrations, like a car driving with a flat tire.

"Helm!" Micky finally called out.

"Thrusters compensating," Clifton yelled as his hands danced across the screens before him.

The ship's flight smoothed for a couple seconds, until the *War Axe* hit the upper atmosphere and started to bounce. This was a critical part of the plan to slow the ship sufficiently to launch the ballistic canister, before reactivating the engines for maximum thrust to slingshot around the planet and head back into space at a speed where the fighters couldn't catch them.

The captain tapped his screen to activate the ship-wide broadcast. "REPORT!" Micky said loudly and firmly. He was the bedrock of the ship, always on display and never allowed to look rattled.

Oscar was the first to speak. "The can is intact and ready to deploy in twelve, eleven..." The next report cut him off.

"Major damage starboard side forward. We're crunched like a Coke can up there. Leaking atmosphere on four decks," Blagun Lagunov reported.

"Two, one, launch," Oscar stated, oblivious to everything else. The bridge crew couldn't tell the can had launched. There was too much turbulence, too many red lights blinking on panels.

"Crew in the areas open to space are accounted for and working to seal the breaches," Mac replied. "No casualties."

"Engines are at full-power. Engaging...now," Suresha reported. The crew were thrust back into their seats. They usually wouldn't feel the acceleration, but the turbulence and damage combined to throw the systems out of sync.

As the *War Axe* climbed, the bouncing and shaking stopped. The forces on their bodies disappeared. Only flashing red lights and the sound of muffled emergency klaxons remained.

1O

Poddern

Terry and Char took point, with Joseph and Petricia by their side. The last Podder they captured walked close behind them. He was unarmed and untethered as he had agreed to come. TH wondered if breaking a promise was something they often did, but Joseph trusted the Podder.

Terry trusted Joseph, and Terry needed to trust the Podder.

The rest of Char's pack was arrayed behind the blue alien. The platoon was spread out behind them and the mechs were far out on the flanks, two to the right and two to the left.

The company hurried to meet the can drop, although Terry wasn't sure how much more ammunition they'd need to accomplish their mission. He finally had a way ahead that made sense to him.

Char wasn't so sure. "These two groups are locked in a

life and death struggle. What's your plan to convince them to lay down arms and play nice?"

"Fear," Terry replied with a wry smile. "They have to fear us more than they fear each other. I don't want to make a show of force, but if they demand that I kill a bunch of them, then that's what I'll do. In the end, it will save lives. Until then, it'll suck for everyone."

Joseph nodded. "I don't think anyone expects anything less, TH."

"Is this what we signed up for, Terry?" Petricia asked. Joseph's wife usually remained quiet. She had been forced against her will to become a vampire those years ago, and she struggled with it. Marrying Joseph had helped, but she still hadn't found a place where she was most comfortable.

She had come along because they both owed Terry Henry their lives. She would stay as long as the debt remained. Joseph said they could leave at any time, but they had no idea where they would go.

"That's a good question," Terry started before taking a deep breath. "No, we didn't, and yes, we did. Wars are messy business. Always. Maybe the Empress thought that we could make them less messy, finish the fight before the people nuked each other into non-existence. I see that as our higher mission. Help expand the Federation, not through conquest, but by getting people to the table.

"Some people only understand force, and we get to pick which side we take. What we're seeing on Poddern is representative of any war I've ever seen or read about. There is no army of the righteous. Only an army. The ones who fight the war are average people who bought into someone else's vision of what had to be done and that violence was the answer."

Terry sighed and looked at the Podder. "You understand me, don't you? You just want to go home to your family."

"I think the same could be said for most of us," Petricia replied. Terry heard the sadness in her voice. With an unintentional glance, Terry confirmed that his children and their spouses were nearby. He didn't have family waiting and wondering. His grandchildren were back on Earth. He missed them, but his closest family was right there.

Family included the vampires, the Were, the warriors. Terry didn't know what to say to Petricia. She didn't expect a reply. Joseph took her hand as they continued toward the canister landing zone.

They'd turned the second Podder loose after Joseph talked with him, apologizing for ripping off two of its tentacles. The Podder seemed unconcerned and said they would grow back.

A streak of fire scarred the heavens. As one, the group on the ground looked up.

"Is that the ship or our can?" Char asked.

"I think that's the *War Axe*," Terry said, squinting into the light. He couldn't make out the ship, only the sign of its passing. A smaller streak appeared behind the ship and raced away from them. "There's our canister. It will loop around on its way here. We better hurry."

THE *WAR AXE*

"Sensors. Don't tell me we're blind," Micky cautioned.

"Okay. I will not tell you," K'Thrall deadpanned. The captain saw the humor, but only shook his head. He'd rather see what was ahead of his ship than have a good laugh.

"Smedley?" the captain asked. "Please display full systems status and projected flight path on the main screen."

The EI complied without responding. Every system on the ship required his presence. He could be everywhere at once, but there was a point where his processes would slow down. He didn't want to risk missing something and have that cost a crewman's life.

The captain unstrapped himself and climbed down from his chair. The *War Axe* was flying true, at least it felt that way. Thrusters were compensating for the damage to the ship's structural integrity.

"Sensors coming back online," K'Thrall noted.

The captain exhaled heavily and watched the screen to see if anything appeared in their flight path. He mumbled to himself. Maybe some thought it was a prayer. Others could have thought it was cheering for the ship and its crew, wishing for the best of luck.

"Flight profile shows clear. We have departed Tissikinnon Four's gravity field. Acceleration is constant. We are on course for Tissikinnon Five," Clifton reported from the helm. He threw his hands up in celebration.

The captain slapped him on the back before making a quick pass around the bridge and thanking everyone. He returned to the captain's chair and activated the ship-wide comm.

"Commander Lagunov, I will meet you forward for an onsite damage assessment. All hands stand down from general quarters and prepare to assist with structural repairs as required. Captain, out."

The captain pulled his hood back and took a deep breath as was his ritual. He stopped, alarm seizing his features. "Smedley, is there a fire somewhere?"

PODDERN

"I don't see it," Terry said. He and Char squinted at the horizon.

It's on its way. Low at eleven o'clock, Kaeden told them. His mech suit had superior optics, beyond the eyes of the merely nanocyte enhanced.

They adjusted where they were looking. "Still don't see it."

Terry's hand rested gently on Char's hip while hers was draped over his shoulder. Joseph and Petricia watched from next to the Podder. Joseph tapped on the alien's shell.

"Is he using Morse code or something like that?" Terry asked.

Petricia stepped up. "He tried to explain that the tapping helps resonate the words that he forms in his mind. He said it was like using a carrier wave, but I don't know what that means."

Terry almost started to explain it, but didn't want to come across as demeaning. Petricia was born after the World's Worst Day Ever, after the fall of mankind. She had been raised in a destroyed world where the only thing that mattered was survival.

"As long as Joseph understands it. I can't thank him enough for helping us to communicate with the locals," Terry replied with a smile.

She looked down shyly.

"And you, too, Petricia. If you hadn't come with us, he would not have either. You are helping to save lives. That may come across as weak since we've already killed so many Podders, but we know that we can do something different now, maybe head off future battles," Terry said softly.

She nodded and put a hand on her husband's shoulder. When she looked up, she smiled proudly.

"Here it comes," Char said. She didn't have to point as the ballistic canister raced toward them. Its stubby wings allowed it to fly parallel to the ground. Small rockets ignited at the last second to slow it down and a second set ignited to help it settle to the ground. It hit with a great thud.

"Woohoo!" Terry shouted. He waved at the others to spread out. They had less than half a mile between them and their resupply.

Secure the site with your mechs, he told Kaeden. Almost immediately, the two on the left started running. The two on the right pushed forward a few moments later.

Do you see the extra suits? Kae asked.

"I'll be damned!" Terry exclaimed. He raised a fist over his head and pumped it up and down, signaling for movement at a double time. "Pick up the pace, people."

Char jogged easily at his side. "You're not getting one of those," she told him.

"Not even for a little while?" Terry asked, knowing that she was right. They'd discussed it and his best place was in managing the battle, not duking it out on the front lines.

"Kimber!" Terry yelled over his shoulder. His daughter quickly caught up to him. "Looks like four more mechs. Take care of manning them, if you would."

"I'll let the four who showed the most promise in the simulator know." She ran off.

"How easy was that?" Char asked as her eyes scanned the area around the canister. She grabbed Terry's arm and slowed. She took a deep breath and bellowed, "LOCK AND LOAD!"

THE WAR AXE

The captain vaulted three steps at a time as he raced downward. He reached the ship's third level and exited the stairwell, running forward along the starboard passageway. Others were running in the same direction.

Micky stepped aside to let the others pass. He stayed far to the right side as he walked forward, looking at this and that. He wanted to be where the damage was right at that moment, but he also didn't want to panic his crew. He pulled his hood on as he approached a closed bulkhead.

Smedley, is this what we're using for an airlock? the captain asked.

>>It is, Captain. As more reports come in, the damage is not as bad as we first thought, but without repairs

done at a shipyard, I fear we won't be able to survive a second attack like that.<<

Micky stopped, stepping into a transverse passage to stay out of the way.

Do you know what hit us?

>>**Commander Lagunov is collecting samples now. I hesitate to guess when we will have a definitive answer soon. There is plenty of debris lodged within the hull from which to make a determination.**<<

Thanks, Smedley. Not that I'm happy to hear about the debris, but I am happy that we're still flying and not in a billion pieces as part of our own debris field. No sense wasting time speculating when there's real work to be done. Open the bulkhead, please.

>>**There is a small repair party coming through. Wait one moment,**<< Smedley replied.

The captain returned to the corridor. When the bulkhead lifted upwards, two crew supported a third between them. The mechanic had a tourniquet around one leg, keeping his ship suit from leaking atmosphere.

There was a jagged cut through the suit and into the man's leg. Micky hurried to pull a stretcher from the wall and set it on the ground. The man winced as he climbed on. The other two crew picked the stretcher up and headed down the connecting corridor where an elevator was located to take them closer to the Pod Doc where the man's leg would get repaired.

Micky watched them go before turning and walking into the space they were using for an airlock. The bulkhead dropped down behind him. When the forward area opened, he saw the chaos beyond.

"My beautiful ship," he whispered.

JOSEPH and the Podder ran past Terry and Char. Timmons hurried forward and took aim, but Terry pushed the barrel of the werewolf's railgun away.

Joseph held up his hands. "He said this is a bad place for a landing!" the vampire yelled over his shoulder. On cue, the can rocked slightly before breaking through the surface and sliding underground.

"No you don't!" Terry yelled and started sprinting. He pulled his Jean Dukes Special, checked the setting with his thumb, and started looking for targets. Terry asked Char out the side of his mouth, "What did you see?"

"A mob of Podders. A big group just below ground level. It's like the can dropped right in the middle of a Pod convention."

Wall-to-wall Podders underground. Follow us in, Kae, Terry passed over his comm chip as he looked around him to see what forces were at his command. werewolves, weretigers, mechs, a platoon of enhanced warriors, and one dog. *Kimber! Secure the can and get your people into those suits. We'll need the firepower, and now would be a good time to get it.*

Terry accelerated as he approached the crater forming around the can. It dropped two meters and then five. Terry launched himself through the air. Char and Dokken followed as they aimed to land atop the canister, between the suits that were latched tightly to the top of what looked like little more than an old Earth shipping crate with wings and an aerodynamic nose cone.

Timmons and Sue were the first to fire into a mass of Podders that appeared from the cave-in. Shonna and Merrit leapt into the crater, sliding to the bottom where they put their backs against the can and fired into the relative dark of the cavern beyond.

Joseph and the Podder captive were next into the hole. The alien slid down the wall on its wide stump-like legs. Joseph fell onto the Podder and hung on to its blue shell as he was dragged downward. Petricia jumped in behind them.

Terry noticed that she didn't have a railgun with her, but he didn't have time to dwell on it. As his eyes adjusted, he saw Podders filling the tunnels that crisscrossed the area just below the surface. The can had landed on top of a broad cavern. The can crashed through as Terry and Char hit, tipped sideways, and then settled right side up.

Terry and Char clung to the armored suits until the can stopped moving. Terry aimed his pistol, then pulled up as Joseph and the Podder ran into his line of fire.

Slugs started impacting around them. Terry took two in the leg and he fell over. Another hit Char in the shoulder, just outside of her ballistic vest. The pistol flew from her numb hand. Slugs slammed into their chests.

"Move, MOVE!" Terry growled as he forced his way over the mech suits and threw himself over the edge. Char dove after him, hitting and rolling, screaming in agony from the damage already done to her body. Her nanocytes were already streaming into the wound.

Dokken landed on top of Terry. TH grunted from the impact. He struggled to stand, using the canister to slide his body upright. The sounds of railguns echoed throughout the chamber.

The werewolves were on the other side. Terry belted out a war cry as he started firing. On the number five setting, he was blowing two Podders backward at a time. He dialed it up to ten.

Char fired her nine-millimeter one-handed with unerring precision. She'd always been the best pistol shot Terry had ever known. She never wavered in combat. He couldn't wait until she carried a JDS.

He hoped they'd survive to see that day.

Blood poured down his shattered leg. More slugs slammed into his body. One bounced off his helmet, shaking his brain and raining sparks before his eyes.

Dokken barked furiously, and then Char went down.

The captain worked his way past the debris in the corridor. When the hull breached, anything not tied down headed toward the breach. The auto-sealing system filled the gap before too much gear was vented to space.

Crew members from all departments were there, forming a chain and moving things out of the way to return the corridor to a certain state of normalcy.

The red emergency lights painted an eerie glow throughout the area.

Smedley, bring up the white lights in this area so we can see what the hell we're doing. At our speed, the chance of a white light giving our position away is irrelevant.

The lights came on, muted at first, and then slowly worked toward full brightness.

The captain spotted his structural department head not far away inspecting the breach into the corridor.

"What do you think?" Micky asked when he arrived.

"I think we scratched the paint on our new ship," Blagun

replied in a loud voice to be heard as he stepped back and put his hands on his hips. He looked unflustered. His hood was in place and his ship suit was clean, unscratched.

"How bad?" Micky was ready for the worst.

Blagun turned toward his captain and cocked his head as if confused. "The *War Axe* was built for this. We're still accelerating into space, flying without any problems. We don't want any more of this garbage." The commander pointed at the split in the hull that destroyed the room beyond and the walls all the way to the hull. "But that doesn't mean we aren't fine. Give my bots a day or two and the breaches will be welded shut. It won't be pretty, but it'll be sound. Just tell me that we're not flying through any more minefields at warp seven and we'll be okay."

"Warp seven?" the captain wondered. "You know it was a minefield?"

"What else would do this?" Blagun looked again at the damage before waving at the captain to follow him. The way forward was crowded with more than debris. The metal bulkheads were twisted and contorted. The two men worked their way around them until they found themselves past the furthest work crew.

They heard the clicks and clacks of a bot installing metal sheeting over a nearby crease. "How many breaches are there?" Micky asked.

Blagun produced a small pad. He tapped it a couple times and then started scrolling. The longer he scrolled, the more the captain's heart sank.

"One hundred and seven, but that's not as bad as it sounds."

"That sounds pretty bad," the captain countered.

"We already have forty-seven of them sealed. We'll have another fifty sealed in an hour. The last ten will take longer," the commander replied.

"What capabilities did we lose?"

"Starboard main weapon is down and can't be repaired. Right now, we can't open the hangar deck to recover the drop ships, but I'm positive that we can fix that ourselves, at least enough to recover the shuttle pods, even if we have to do it one at a time through a half-open door. As long as you give me a week to make the repairs," Blagun said, raising one eyebrow.

"We need to be able to recover them whenever they're ready. Since it'll take three days for us to slow down, turn around, and head back to the planet, you have that long to get one of the hangar bay doors operational. We may have more time, but don't count on it."

The captain wasn't kidding. He was still angry about the destruction to his ship by what should have been a marginally capable space force.

"*You* can count on us. *They* can count on us. It'll be ready when they are," the commander promised.

The captain turned and walked away, refusing to look further at the damage to his ship because he could do nothing about it, and he was holding up the people who could.

TERRY FIRED his JDS as quickly as he could recover his aim

after each trigger pull. He fired in a pattern, blasting swaths of blue aliens from the connected tunnels.

Suddenly, there were no more slugs flying in his direction. He struggled forward, his leg still damaged. He needed to buy time for his body to repair itself. A slug had hit his neck and blood was running freely down his chest. He slapped a free hand over the wound and struggled one-legged over the rubble until he got to Char. Dokken was standing between her and the closest tunnel, growling at the darkness beyond.

Terry fell over the last rocks, landing heavily next to Char. There was a crease across her forehead where a slug had hit. Terry checked the wound.

It hadn't penetrated. Char groaned as Terry pulled her roughly to him. Her shoulder was torn up. Her ballistic vest was destroyed. Blood covered her face.

Terry couldn't pull her to her feet because he wasn't able to stand. *Kaeden. We need you. We're both down on the starboard side of the can.*

On my way, Kaeden replied.

Railguns continued to fire rapidly from the other side. Pings from slugs hitting the canister pounded out an ear-splitting staccato. Terry held Char and rocked. Dokken started to bark.

Terry fired blindly into the tunnel. Three shots, left to right. Dokken settled down.

"Do you see anything?" Terry asked in a normal voice.

They're down there. I can smell them, Dokken replied.

Terry looked at his leg. The wound was closed, but he couldn't put any weight on it. He let go of the wound on his neck. It too had sealed. He pulled his canteen and took a long drink. He almost jumped out of his skin when the mech slammed into the ground less than a meter in front of him. Dokken bolted into the tunnel, but quickly returned.

"Nice entrance," Terry told the back of the suit.

The ground shook three more times as the mechs arrived within the tunnel.

Expand the perimeter and then let's get those mechs unbolted, Terry broadcasted using his comm chip. He was starting to get the hang of using it. Instantaneous command and control for a unit no matter the size. He had thought it would come in handy, but now he was positive.

Kaeden stepped past the German Shepherd and headed into the tunnel. His large railgun cracked rapidly, unleashing its full destructive power against a relatively defenseless enemy. The mech backed up and assumed a defensive position, the railgun swinging menacingly back and forth.

"Where's Joseph?" Terry bellowed. *Where's Joseph?*

"Over here, Terry!" Timmons yelled from the other side of the can.

We have a problem, Joseph told Terry using his comm chip.

Explain.

My friend here says this is a bad Pod. His Pod is at war with this one, Joseph explained.

How in the fuck does that work? Tell him to tell this Pod that they are all going to die if they keep coming at us.

Can't do it, TH. He doesn't speak their language.

He's a Podder. How can he not speak Podder? What in the jump the fuck up and down has he been speaking with you? Terry tried to stand because he wanted to look Joseph in the face for this conversation. He couldn't believe what he was hearing.

Telepathy is different, but Podders are like humans. They grow up in different areas, speak different languages. How's your French?

Don't fuck with me, Joseph. You have got to be shitting me. Why didn't he tell us they were in the middle of a civil war?

That's probably my fault. I thought I understood what he was saying, but there's a lot of nuance. Joseph and the Podder appeared around the front of the can and approached Terry. "My bust, TH."

Terry looked at the vampire and the Podder captive. "If he's not with them, then why did he run when the can fell through the crust?"

"He was trying to stop us from getting into the middle of the bad guys. His words, Terry." Joseph held his hands up in surrender.

"Our Podder can't talk with these Podders, but that's okay, because his Pod is at war with these. I expect these are the ones that killed the Crenellians, but since they can't tell the Podders apart, they're killing all Podders. So how can *we* tell them apart?" Terry wondered.

Joseph tapped on the Podder's shell, nodded, then tapped some more.

Terry waited patiently, willing time to pass more quickly so his leg would heal enough that he could stand up and go hit something. Char stirred, struggling to open her eyes. Her pupils were dilated as she fought against the pain within her head.

"He said the bad ones are blue," Joseph said cautiously.

"Goddammit, Joseph! Now I know you're fucking with me. They're *all* BLUE!"

"I know, I know. He tried to describe the difference, but imagine using words to tell the difference between sky blue and robin's egg blue."

"Is there a difference?" Terry asked.

"For a snappy dresser like you? Probably not. Felicity could probably tell the difference."

A mech from the other side of the can opened fire. Joseph's eyes darted toward the sound of the railgun.

KIMBER ARRAYED the platoon outside the crater. She heard the fire, saw the slugs ricocheting off the can. She couldn't see clearly through the dust and debris into the darkness below to see how the Bad Company was faring. The volume of fire from both sides was deafening.

When the Jean Dukes Special opened up, the entire dynamic changed. Podder slug-throwers were mostly silenced. Railguns sent darts at hypervelocity into the tunnels. The echoes died away into an eerie silence.

"Dad?"

She heard his call for Kaeden to help and breathed a sigh of relief. Cory and Ramses tried to get past her and into the hole. Kimber held them back.

"I don't think the battle's over down there. Wait until Kae and the armor boys get into place." Kimber had a firm grip on Cory's arm. Her blue eyes flashed angrily for a moment, but she understood.

"Let me know as soon as I can go. I think Mom and Dad are both injured. They need me," she pleaded.

"I can't imagine anyone down there who isn't injured." Kim craned her neck to look from one warrior to the next. "Gomez, Kelly, Capples, Fleeter, get in the hole and bring those suits to life."

"Yes, ma'am!" came a chorus of replies. Two men and two women jogged to the edge of the hole, assessing the distance to jump to the top of the canister before determining that it was too far.

Kim pointed to the side where a slope led into the hole. The werewolves had taken that way in.

The four jumped over the edge one after the other, sliding into the cavern below. They hit the bottom, came to their feet, and raced to the can, where they used the stubby wings to help them climb to the top of the canister where the suits were affixed. They each took one, studying how the suits were held in place.

Capples took charge and directed the four to clear one suit at a time and then the first into the suit could expedite unhooking the others.

Do you need more manpower? I have a platoon up here itching to get into the fight, Kimber asked.

Soon. We're expanding the perimeter now. Get this, these are different Podders than the others and the two factions are at war, Terry explained.

Kimber mulled over what the colonel had said. *They're both shooting at us, then. Is there anyone here who doesn't want to shoot at us?*

Before Terry could answer, Auburn appeared and

started to climb into the hole. "Where the hell are you going?" Kimber asked abruptly.

He caught himself as he was hanging halfway over the edge. "I'm in charge of logistics and our resupply is right there." Auburn pointed with his off-hand, almost losing his grip on the edge. "I'm going to see what we have and start the distribution. So what if we're in the middle of the shit? That's when our people need the supplies the most."

He looked determined. Kimber had encouraged him to get enhanced because she didn't want to watch him grow old and die. He didn't want that either, so he went into the Pod Doc. He wasn't military and never would be. He had been a rancher. So he became master of the supply chain.

That had been seventy years earlier. He had his job and that helped the warriors do theirs. He took his logistics job seriously because he still had no intention of carrying a rifle. Auburn reasoned that if he didn't contribute in the way that worked for him, he'd be on the outside looking in. A long life as an outcast wasn't what he had in mind when he agreed to get enhanced.

"Let me go, Kim. It's what I need to do," he told his wife. Kim felt the vibrations of the mechs under her brother's command. Each vaulted into the cavern. Kae headed into a tunnel and opened up with his mech-sized railgun. The others took their positions around the can.

"Do your thing, Auburn," she told him with a smile. His white teeth gleamed against his dark skin, before he let go, turned, and slid into the cavern. He was running before he hit the bottom. He looped around the wing to get to the can's aft access door.

Auburn cranked the doors open to find the canister chocked full of supplies. Water trickled out between the crates and out the door to disappear into the dry dirt of the cavern.

Two warriors appeared behind Auburn, their backs to him and their weapons aimed into the darkness. Cory rushed past with Ramses by her side.

The *War Axe*

Micky San Marino stood in the engine compartment and reveled at the power that his ship generated. Gravitic drives for normal flight. The gate engine that established a wormhole while simultaneously stabilizing the event horizon for a smooth transition from normal space.

So much power at his command. The power got the ship into trouble and the power helped it escape. The engines themselves were located centrally within the hull to minimize the risk of damage to irreplaceable components. Becoming stranded in deep space was a death sentence.

Commander Suresha waited. She was in no hurry. Everything on her end was humming right along even with half her people chopped to Blagun's structural repair teams.

A movement in a side alcove drew both their attention. Clodagh Shortall walked out, carrying Wenceslaus and lovingly stroking his head. When she saw the captain and the commander, she dropped the cat. With a yowl, the good king landed on his feet. He continued to berate her in the language of his people, until he saw that he was being watched.

He faced the captain, stood on his back legs for a moment, batted the air with his paws, and bolted.

"CLODAGH!" Micky yelled and started running. Her eyes shot wide and she took off after the cat.

The captain stopped and turned back to Suresha. "You knew about this," he said accusingly.

"I don't follow," Suresha said, pursing her lips to whistle before pointing at the engines. "These could be the best performing engines in the whole fleet!"

She bobbed her head excitedly.

"Of course they are." The captain didn't look where the department head was pointing. "Clodagh brought that cat aboard, didn't she?"

"I can't say for sure, but I suspect there may have been some complicity with elements, *not me*, in regards to the feline nature of a certain crew member's affinity where work always come first for a place that we call home…"

Micky held up his hand, signaling for Suresha to stop. "What is that? You're just stringing words together that make no sense. A simple yes or no would suffice."

Suresha refused to look at the captain, puffing out her cheeks as she kept her mouth shut.

Micky started to laugh and then stopped. "I almost destroyed the ship today," he said, turning serious. "But the crew saved her, because we don't just have the best engines, we have the best crew in the fleet. So, if Clodagh wants to keep a cat, that's fine. Tell her to keep the little bastard out of my quarters."

Suresha shook her head just enough to tell the captain that she wasn't going to do that.

"Off my bed, then?" he negotiated.

She didn't move.

"Fine," Micky conceded. "Is there anything you need from me to keep the engines humming?"

"Whatever the ship ran into? Please, don't run into any more of that. We need to repair a few of the gate emitters before we can gate out of here. The engine is fine, but the emitters are located on the hull. But they should be repaired within a day. I've dispatched two bots to make the repairs, then another day aligning and testing. We'll have full gate capability two days from now."

"Next time, start with that," Micky said, smiling. He headed toward the door, looking over his shoulder as he went. "I wasn't blowing smoke when I said we have the best crew in the fleet. I honestly believe it because we have department heads who lead from the front."

COMMANDER OSCAR WIRTH studied the display in his office located next to the main fabrication area. Data from the canister was being transmitted continuously. He was reading the damage reports and gear statuses.

The can landed without issue, but afterwards, it had been perforated repeatedly by something. Some of the water stores were impacted, some of the food. The ammunition was fine, like Char's nine-millimeter, whose cartridges were contained in a double-walled metal container.

The biggest question surrounded the rockets, which took up a third of the can because of the excess packaging around them. The armored suits needed them as the only long-range engagement weapon in Terry Henry's arsenal.

Auburn had directed that they would take less food to make sure they received a full stock of rockets. Oscar refused to do that, so he used pre-packaged food as stuffing between the weapons.

He was dismayed at the loss of water. A number of the bulk containers within had been penetrated and were leaking. Auburn ordered water as if there were no potable sources on the planet.

Oscar had no idea what was available on the planet. "I need to be more involved with the planning," he told himself. He had met with Auburn before the Bad Company launched, but he hadn't fully embraced the forward thinking it took for an operation in unknown territory, surrounded by hostile forces.

"If we didn't have to make that run, the ship wouldn't be broken and water wouldn't be leaking out of my canister," he said. Oscar ran a finger over his screen. "Are we going to get my can back?"

He shook his head, believing that the canister had become a permanent fixture on Tissikinnon Four. He hoped none of the other equipment would join it.

PODDERN

The four mechs holding the perimeter opened fire together. They fired, advanced three steps, and fired again.

Kelly stood in her powered, armored suit atop the can and fired slowly, but steadily, turning in a circle. The other three working to free the next suit ducked their heads and covered their ears.

She stopped firing and quickly unlatched the next suit. Fleeter crawled in, laying on her face as it buttoned up behind her. Gomez took the next one.

By the time he was in, Fleeter was crawling unsteadily to her feet. Together, they finished preparing the last suit, even standing it up to make it easier on Capples.

He climbed in and started the diagnostics process. Kelly moved to the front of the can, aimed, and fired. With one jump, she vaulted into the cavern.

"Reporting for duty," she said using her suit's external speakers.

"Join Praeter and watch his back," Kae ordered. On the heads-up display within the helmets, the other suits were detailed by who was in them. It made coordinating effortless.

Kae directed Gomez, Fleeter, and Capples into similar backup roles. Kelly followed Kaeden into the tunnel, moving deliberately, scanning, looking, and firing when needed.

CORY HAD PUT one hand on her father's leg and one on her mother's forehead. With a great effort, she helped their nanocytes to hasten the healing process.

Char's breathing slowed and her eyes cleared. Terry flexed and stretched. Ramses had his arm wrapped around Cory's waist. He held his railgun in the other hand, looking for enemies at the edges of the cavern.

Terry Henry Walton stood up straight, clenching his fists. "I hate getting shot," he declared.

Char looked at him with one raised eyebrow. "I'm pretty sure that goes for all of us," she said. They turned to see Auburn working his way toward them through the rubble.

"We lost some water, but everything else looks to be intact. We can set up a chain and move the supplies out of the hole. It won't take too long," Auburn told them.

"Joseph," Terry called. The vampire and the Podder had moved to a cavern wall away from two open tunnels. They looked to be hanging out.

Joseph leaned around the tunnel saw the dim lights from a mech in the distance. He brushed himself off and walked confidently toward TH.

As he approached, they saw that he'd been riddled with Podder slugs. Dried blood left spots and trails all over his body. Cory's eyes drooped, but she reached out to help him regardless.

He smiled and intercepted her hand, turning it over, and kissing the back softly. "No, my dear. I'm fine. Time heals all wounds, or so they say."

Petricia had been crouching between the Podder and the wall. They didn't see her until the blue alien moved, at which time they saw that she'd also been shot, and more than once.

She stayed behind the alien as it approached, leaning its stalk-head closer to Joseph.

"Looks like you have a new buddy," Terry said, but not in a harsh way. The Podder's shell was dinged and scratched from all the slugs that had hit it. Its stalk had been damaged from other impacts.

Cory started to climb up the alien's shell, but Ramses held her back. After a short argument that ended with a kiss, he helped her up. The alien remained still as she put her hands on the worst of the wounds.

Joseph tapped the creature's shell.

Cory moved her hand swiftly from wound to wound, giving a measured amount of herself to each, healing none of them completely before moving on. The blue glow of her eyes dimmed and then her lids fluttered closed. Ramses had been ready and caught her as she rolled off the alien.

Joseph smiled and stopped tapping. "It was like looking at something through a heavy fog, and all of a sudden, the fog lifts. I can hear Bundin clearly now. That's his name. He expresses his appreciation for the relief. He said the injuries were causing him extreme pain."

"They can feel pain?" Terry asked.

"Yes, they are very sensitive. The neck and tentacles are mostly one nerve bundle that funnels sensory input to the brain. When you shoot what you call the stalk, it causes them so much pain that they expire. Not blood loss, not organ damage, but the agony of the injury is what kills them."

Terry looked down and sighed. Nearly every Podder he'd killed had been because of shooting its stalk. He'd tortured them to death. No wonder they fought like demons, forcing him to kill even more of them.

"Then why did they attack us in the first place?" Terry asked through clenched teeth.

"They thought we were a new Crenellian attack. Bundin holds no grudge. They did what they thought they had to, and we did what we had to. Now we know better."

"I wish I had his sense of logic. I'm going to feel horrible for who knows how long. Thanks for making me feel like shit, but that's not what I wanted to ask."

Terry walked forward to check on Cory. She was asleep in Ramses's arms. He'd positioned himself behind the Podder, so none of the tunnels had a direct view of them, just in case the aliens fired their slug-throwers in the can's direction. Terry saw Char's pistol on the ground.

He picked it up.

TH turned back to Joseph. "Do we fight our war above ground or underground?"

"Good question," the vampire replied. He communicated with the alien without having to tap. Cory's nanocytes sped up the healing process, and also aligned their thoughts to allow Joseph to better understand what the alien was saying.

Joseph continued, "Bundin says that everything on this planet happens underground. If we want to talk with the Podders, it would be down here. If we want to find the Crenellians, down here. If we want to accomplish any of our mission objectives, that will be done down here," Joseph explained before adding helpfully, "At least we won't be on the receiving end of more Podder artillery."

"That answers my question," Terry said, before looking

at Auburn. "We'll unload the can, resupply and rearm down here, and will conduct the next phase of the operations in these tunnels."

Kimber, bring everyone into the cavern. This will be our launching point. Tell everyone to say good-bye to the sun, Terry ordered.

KAEDEN HAD the path he'd taken mapped to his HUD. He could find his way back, at least for now. Kelly had his back, which gave him confidence as he moved forward.

There had been some resistance initially, but the Podders had fled when they realized the mech was impervious to their attacks.

Which made Kaeden even more cautious. The Podders had huge artillery pieces that they'd used against the Bad Company. He expected the enemy wasn't retreating, but were reorganizing around heavier firepower.

The suit was not too much bigger than a human. The driver's movements were mirrored and magnified. There was no exposed skin. He was completely protected, unless an artillery round slammed him into the wall. A certain amount of kinetic energy could be blocked and absorbed, but beyond that, the suit's wearer could be subjected to stresses beyond what the body could survive.

In those cases, the suit would double as a coffin.

Kae held up his fist, and he listened. Kelly took one more step and froze. The Podders didn't make any noise when they moved, but something was making noise up ahead, the sound of leather being dragged against stone.

Kaeden inched forward, until he reached the next intersection. Even though he had the suit on the highest light magnification, he couldn't see anything. He switched to IR before he leaned around the corner.

Ten meters away, a mob of Podders were pushing two small humanoids before them.

Dad, I think we've found a couple Crenellians. It seems like the Pod is trying to use them as shields.

Once the fighting started, Marcie had grabbed Aaron, Yanmei, Christina, and their four warriors and headed out, looking for an alternate entrance to the caves and tunnels below.

She fumed at the situation, understanding every bit what Terry Henry Walton was putting himself through.

She heard the withering fire from within the cavern and then it was silenced by an enfilade from the Jean Dukes Special and the werewolves' railguns.

Marcie chuckled to herself. "Say 'hello' to the Bad Company, bitches." She reached into the Etheric, drew power from it, and let the landscape before her ghost through the mists.

The dimension fed power to her nanocytes and gave her strength with which to see, see that the Podders registered as almost nonexistent. The enhanced members of the company burned like beacons in the darkness. And far down the valley there was something else, a different presence.

"Follow me!" Marcie called and started to run, using all of her enhanced strength to accelerate to an inhuman pace. Railguns cracked from the cavern behind her, quieter as the distance increased. Aaron and Yanmei sprinted. Jones growled as he encouraged the others to pick up their pace.

The four warriors had been enhanced on the ship in transit from Earth to the Dren Cluster. They were unpracticed at extreme speed running, but what they lacked in experience, they made up for with sheer determination.

Marcie pushed as fast as she could go, not bothering to look over her shoulder. With her enhanced hearing, she could hear them all. She enjoyed nearly vampiric speed, with the strength of a Werebear and refined vision to see more sharply into the Etheric. She trained every day, her mind and her body. She sparred with anyone who would face her.

She was fearless, but understood Terry's challenge to win without fighting. "Someday, you may be at peace with your enemies. Make sure you can look them in the face, and not down on them."

Honor. Courage. Commitment. The three words that Terry had preached for all her life. He sold everyone he met on the premise of those three words.

Fight with honor, in a cause worth fighting for.

Initially, she couldn't embrace the fact that the Force de Guerre had been split up, one half to create the foundation of the FDG, a Federation-sanctioned special military force. The other half was the Bad Company, a mercenary outfit.

Fighting for money, but also fighting to expand the Federation.

Each client presented a new opportunity to increase Federation influence and security. Nathan wanted Tissikinnon Four to be at peace with its neighboring system so both planets would expand the buffer to the unknown.

The best part was that the Crenellians were paying the Bad Company to do what the Federation wanted. It made for an economically viable Federation growth strategy.

It also pissed Marcie off that they were in the middle of a bad situation that seemed to be turning worse.

She slowed the group as they approached a cut into a small hill. Marcie stopped and examined the area. She closed her eyes and looked around her using the power of the Etheric. She found a space beneath her feet and there were a number of people there. She saw a small tunnel hidden within the cut.

"Lock and load, people," she said, checking her railgun. She was low on ammunition and did not have another magazine of darts. "How are we doing on ammo?"

Aaron and Yanmei both gave a thumbs up. Christina returned a thumbs down. The other four shook their heads. Two were carrying their combat knives because their weapons were empty.

"Give those two your thundersticks and packs. Do what you do best," she said, looking at Aaron, Yanmei, and Christina. They instantly handed their railguns to the two warriors.

Aaron and Yanmei stripped out of their clothes and changed into weretiger form. Christina changed into a werewolf, not a Pricolici. Marcie looked confused. "I didn't know you could do that," Marcie admitted.

The werewolf pulled its lips back in a version of the canine smile. She still looked terrifying, as werewolves did. Marcie pointed to two of the warriors. "Up front with me, then you—" She pointed at the Were. "—and then you two bringing up the rear. There are Crenellians in here. They are the ones who hired us, but just in case this bunch didn't get the word, let's try not to kill any of them."

She turned and walked slowly into the cut, looking for the entrance she knew was there. She wasn't disappointed in how well hidden it was. The dirt had been smoothed over top, blending it with the surroundings.

Marcie looked around her. "Someone did this from the outside," she said softly. She tipped her chin toward the sides of the small ravine and the two weretigers leapt into action. Aaron vaulted to the hill on the left, ran to the top, and then followed the ridge line up and away from where the others. Yanmei did the same thing on the right side. Christina ran straight ahead, following the ravine's meandering course.

The others took a knee and watched. The Were soon returned, joining Marcie near the hidden doorway. She couldn't talk with them in that form, but their body language said that they'd found nothing. Aaron dropped and rolled in the dirt. Christina joined him, filling her coat with dust. She stood and shook, sending a cloud of dirt through the air. Yanmei laid down and watched the antics.

Marcie kicked the dirt away from the hatch that was set at an angle into the hillside. She cleared the door, then spun the handle, surprised that it hadn't been locked.

The two warriors took their positions next to the door, ready to jump through and to the side as soon as it was opened. Marcie's muscles tightened and she jerked the door open.

The two warriors dove into a dimly lit tunnel, hit the hard dirt floor, and rolled to both sides. They came up into firing positions and looked down the empty tunnel, lit by a string of lights overhead.

Marcie peeked around the door before walking cautiously inside. She looked for traps, including some of the high-tech devices she'd seen on the ship like lasers or motion sensors. But the walls were plain, carved from the rock.

She worked her way slowly down the tunnel. The two warriors stood and followed, looking over the barrels of their railguns as they moved, taking care to keep their lines of fire clear.

The Were followed Marcie in and the last two warriors stayed at the door, watching the approach within the ravine.

"Hey!" someone yelled from ahead as soon as Marcie rounded a corner and saw what looked like a low-tech operations center. Computers and monitors were arranged in a circle around an open area where a small humanoid stood on a low platform.

He looked at her without fear. None of them seemed to have weapons. Marcie stopped where the tunnel opened into the space. She counted a dozen Crenellians.

"I suspect you are the hired help?" the man in the center said, putting his hands on his hips, assuming a human pose of disdain and dominance.

Marcie instantly didn't like him.

"I'm Colonel Marcie Walton from the Bad Company and we'd like to have a few words, if you don't mind."

"You shut up," the man said before she finished. "You'll do what you're told, what you're paid for, if the pea brain inside that giant body of yours can register what I'm saying."

"STAY THERE!" Terry yelled before switching to his comm chip. *Stay there.*

"Char and Joseph, follow me. Everyone else, get those supplies distributed. We'll rally up here as soon as possible," Terry explained as he started walking toward the tunnel that Kaeden had disappeared into.

Hold positions. Maintain the perimeter as is. Timmons, rearm your team first and then provide security as the platoon loads up. Build a plan to demo the tunnels to protect our rear and flanks. Terry issued his orders as he walked into the darkness. He hated to do it, but after the first corner, the darkness was near absolute.

He pulled a flashlight from his pack, turned it on, and shined it ahead of him. The tunnels were a combination of natural and Podder-made. They'd built an entire civilization underground.

Terry was hurrying, but slowed down. His own adage was "don't be in a hurry to your own funeral."

"What do they eat?" Terry asked.

Joseph shrugged. "I got the impression that they had vast mushroom farms or something that looked like mushrooms. There is water here, caverns filled with crystal clear water. Underground springs and rivers. There's water above ground, too. We just happened to land in a desert area."

Terry looked behind him and saw the Podder following. "Did you tell him he could come?"

Joseph shook his head. "He's free, remember?" Joseph replied.

"I guess it's okay, as long as he doesn't reignite his civil war against the blue pod."

"Now you understand!" Joseph answered with a big smile.

Terry wasn't sure he understood anything. He didn't know why the Podder was coming along because he couldn't speak with the other Podders and didn't like the Crenellians. Maybe he felt safe with the vampire.

"Don't let him start a firefight. If anyone is going to make this thing go south, it'll be me." Terry looked at Char to find her nodding. She stopped when the light showed her face. She shook her head and made a sour face.

"Nothing of the sort, lover," she said, trying to sound supportive. Terry turned back to look down the tunnel. He could see Kelly ahead. Her armored suit still had scorch marks from where the canister burned its way through the atmosphere.

Terry, Char, Joseph, and Bundin moved past the stationary mech. Kelly nodded from the other side of her face shield. Kaeden leaned around a corner not far ahead.

"Coming up behind you," Terry said calmly.

"Don't get past me. There's an army up here."

The four slowed as they approached. Terry called for

the group to stop. He moved in behind the mech and leaned around to shine his flashlight and get a look at the tactical situation.

"Well now, that sucks," he said, seeing the condition of the two Crenellians and the sea of waving blue stalk-heads behind them.

All movement stopped. Terry looked over his shoulder and saw Bundin standing there. "How can you move so quietly?" Terry wondered aloud. He turned back to the standoff.

"I'm open to suggestions," he said.

Char and Joseph squeezed in beside Kaeden. Joseph reached out with his mind, but quickly drew back. "There are too many of them. The sound of their minds is deafening."

"What about our two buddies up front? They speak a language we understand."

Joseph refocused his efforts. "They're terrified," he said as he intently watched the two men. "They've been captives for a little under two days. It seems they were taken about the time we landed. I expect the Podders saw our arrival as an escalation in the conflict."

"It was," Terry admitted. "It still is, but we don't need to kill anymore, prefer not to kill anymore, but we will if we have to. Can you convey that to the blue Podders?"

"I cannot. I can hear the Crenellians, but not those who hold them captive," Joseph replied.

One of the Podders moved forward and shoved two slug-throwers against the Crenellians head.

"What's it want us to do, Joseph?" Terry asked.

"No idea. Bundin?" Joseph put a hand on the Podder's shell. "He said the man will die if we do not leave."

Terry was about to ask how Bundin knew, but the blue Podder's slug-thrower popped and the man's head exploded. He flopped to the ground, spasmed twice, and became still.

"Makes me want to kill them all, again," Terry said. He hadn't flinched when the prisoner was executed, only drilled in on the one who'd done the execution. He slowly pulled his JDS and aimed. "The question is, can we cause enough chaos to rescue the other one or do we retreat?"

The Podder aimed at the second Crenellian.

"If he kills that one, we will slather these walls with blue blood," Terry growled, before stepping out from behind the mech and shouting. "I don't like being threatened."

Terry took aim at the Podder and walked forward. Kae slapped his railgun as he aimed into the blue mass. Char aimed her pistol. Even Joseph pulled his railgun around the front and prepared to fire.

The blue stalks were frozen like stalagmites as Terry walked forward, his pistol aimed unwaveringly at the alien's stalk. Terry checked the setting with his thumb. It was still at ten.

At eleven, I could completely clear this tunnel, he thought. He prepared to adjust, should the enemy kill the prisoner. *Before the Crenellian's blood splatters the wall, the blue sea will part.*

But the shot did not come. Terry reached the prisoner, grabbed his arm, and pulled him away. The Podder continued to aim at the man's head. Terry backed up, dragging the man with him. After the death of his countryman, the Crenellian had become a quivering mass. Terry wasn't certain, but he thought the man may have soiled himself.

He couldn't blame him. Terry didn't know if this captive was a miner or a soldier.

Probably not a soldier. The man looked weak and not dressed for war. If he was a soldier, then Terry knew why the Crenellians had hired the Bad Company.

When a job needs to be done right, hire professionals.

Terry rounded the corner and handed the Crenellian to Char and Joseph. They pulled him out of sight of the Podders. Terry dialed the JDS to eleven and braced himself.

"Do it," Kaeden whispered.

Terry wanted to, but he didn't want to. There was only one Podder who deserved justice. He dialed it back to a setting of two. "When I fire, you bring the ceiling down right in front of us," Terry said.

Kae raised his weapon. Maybe the Podders thought they were safe. Terry fired once and blew the entire stalk off the Podder who had executed the captive. Kae instantly zipped one hundred hypervelocity darts across the ceiling. The rumble told everyone that the tunnel was caving in. Terry ran and Kaeden backed up.

Slug-throwers barked, but in moments, it was over. Dust filled the air and the silence returned. The tunnel was closed.

Terry walked up to the Crenellian. He had both his hands over his head. Char shook her head, just a little.

"I need you to tell us what you know so we can end this war," Terry told the man, pleading for him to come back to himself.

The small man kept his head covered with his hands.

He was bald, as had been the other Crenellian. The president had worn a head covering of sorts.

Maybe they were all bald. His size reminded Terry of a twelve-year-old boy. Thin and frail-looking. Head a little bigger than a human's with small bumps for ears, without ear holes. Terry wondered if they could hear the same low frequency where the Podders communicated.

"Let's get you back into the sunlight," Terry told the man. He wouldn't move, so Terry picked up him. The Crenellian wrapped his arms around Terry's neck and buried his head in Terry's chest.

Kelly led the way up the tunnel while Kae walked backwards in case the blue Pod broke through.

In between, Terry, Char, and Joseph were accompanied by two aliens who were at war with each other as well as themselves.

"Can this get any more fucked up?" Terry asked.

14

Marcie turned to the warriors beside her. They were still aiming their railguns, but both men only had one target. She smiled knowing that if they pulled the triggers, the arrogant little prick would be blown into next week along with half the wall behind him.

She signaled for them to lower their weapons.

She walked forward casually, taking stock of what she saw on the computer screens until those at the consoles closed their displays, as if afraid to reveal secrets to the enemy. She walked up to the man and loomed over him.

"I think we got off on the wrong foot somehow. Let me…"

"I don't care what you have to say," the Crenellian interrupted again. In less than a blink of an eye, Marcie had the man by the throat and lifted into the air.

"You little shit. You're going to fucking listen," she growled, giving the alien time to gurgle but not releasing any pressure on his throat so he could talk.

He kicked her in the stomach. She was wearing her ballistic vest and could hardly feel it. Marcie slammed his feet into the ground, lifted him up, and slammed him again. She put him down gently after that, but kept her fingers wrapped around his throat.

She thought for a moment that she could understand the Crenellian as if he was speaking English. She appreciated the technology for a moment, before returning to the matter at hand.

"The landing coordinates *you* gave us sucked. They had nothing to do with what you hired us for. It appeared that you wanted to use our firepower for the genocide of your enemy. Guess what, cheesedick? Our mission is to end this war, which is what we're going to do, but we think we can accomplish that by removing your dumb asses since you're the ones stirring the pot. That's what I see anyway."

The weretigers and werewolf strolled into the chamber, casually sniffing each of the Crenellians. The man in the center massaged his throat and watched the beasts closely.

They converged on him all at once as if by design. Aaron bared his fangs and Christina growled. Yanmei opened her mouth above his head, letting cat drool drip onto his bald pate.

He ducked away and wiped his head with an arm, keeping it there to protect his face.

"It's about time you showed us a little respect. You want us to do your dirty work for you. You have the gall to look down on us? In order to get back into my good graces, you need to tell me who you are and give me a tour so I can see what's going on."

"If I refuse," he managed to rasp.

"Then we drag all your asses into the daylight and throw you into the middle of the Podder army. I see that you aren't packing any heat. You may not last long."

"Who are the Podders?"

"You call them the Tiskers, but that's not what they call themselves. Have you never talked with them?" she asked.

"How were we supposed to talk with them? They don't speak," the man retorted, still rubbing his throat but getting his arrogance back. Aaron showed his fangs before rubbing his cat face on the man's head, putting his scent on him.

"And you had the nerve to call me a dumbass. Of course they speak, just not in a way that you understand. We've been able to communicate with them," Marcie explained, continuing to loom over the alien. "Tour time, dickhead."

"No." He crossed his arms and tipped his chin back, looking more like a petulant child than a leader. Marcie nodded to Christina.

The werewolf rammed the Crenellian, knocking him to the ground. She straddled him, growling and snapping at his face.

Dad, we found a Crenellian outpost not far from the cavern. They are uncooperative, to say the least, but I expect they'll come around before I run out of cards to play, Marcie reported using her comm chip.

"You—" Marcie pointed to one of the aliens sitting at a computer terminal. "Tell me what you do."

WHEN TERRY RETURNED to the chamber, he found the distribution of ammunition, food, and water well under way.

"Status?" Terry asked Auburn.

"We'll finish in a couple minutes. Most of the can was filled with rockets, food packs stuffed in between, nevertheless..." Auburn trailed off as someone handed him a pouch.

He peeked inside before passing them to Char. "Extra magazines and ammunition." She thanked him as she took it and looked for a place to sit to reload her empties.

Terry's JDS reload was in his pack and he didn't think he'd need to reload for this operation or maybe the next ten operations. The firepower in that pistol was earthshaking. He appreciated it more and more whenever he thought about it.

He'd keyed it to his hand as well as any of his family. When the next one was ready, he'd give that to Marcie, then Kimber, then Ramses. He had his list of priorities. Not just anyone could fire a JDS. If someone wasn't careful, the pistols had a way of ripping their arm off.

ONE OF THE warriors handed Terry three bags, two with water and one with food. Char received her resupply. She immediately downed one of the water containers, a thin foil pouch. Once finished, she folded the pouch and put it back in the bag.

The rule that if you packed it in, you need to pack it out applied, even if you were on a different planet.

Terry stayed out of the way of the efficient resupply. He gave Kimber the thumbs up.

Joseph was talking with the Podder with Petricia by his side. The freed captive was huddled against the wall.

The four werewolves—Timmons, Sue, Shonna, and Merrit—were eating as if starving. Timmons threw a wrapper on the ground. Terry stared at him until he picked it up and stuffed it in his pocket.

Marcie called when he started to wonder where she was, along with Christina.

Terry nodded as he talked using the comm chip. Char looked up, wondering with whom he was communicating. She didn't have long to wait to find out.

"Marcie found some Crenellians. She says that she's talking with the little pricks right now."

"As friendly and forthcoming as the president?" Char teased.

"That's my impression. A race of dicks." Terry kicked at the ground before sitting beside his wife.

"Is it the headquarters we've been looking for?" Char took a bite of something and made a face, but continued to chew.

"She used the term outpost, so I don't think so, but they'll know where it is." Terry drank one of his packets of water and opened a meal bar. "We'll turn that one back over to his fellow Crenellians as soon as possible. If she's talking with them, then we don't need what he knows, which I don't think will be much."

Auburn joined Terry and Char. Kimber was setting the watch, making sure one group of her people had been fed and were on watch before the second group started to eat.

Four of the mechs were open with their people taking a break. The other four were on watch.

Terry didn't expect an attack at that moment, but being ready was one thing that he trained all of his people for. He ate and drank with his left hand while keeping his right near his pistol.

Always.

Char's eyes darted around, as did Terry's, looking for anything that shouldn't have been there. Just in case.

"Auburn, can you set up the comm, please? I need to report in."

Auburn stuffed the rest of the food bar into his mouth and chewed as he removed the equipment from his pack. He chewed the entire time he set up the comm system, including activating the Etheric power source to drive the signal across the universe.

Terry and Char were mesmerized. Terry had to ask, "Are you ever going to finish chewing?"

"It's like trying to eat a clot of dried glue," he shared as he signaled that the communication system was live.

Terry stood before talking. It was his way. Auburn adjusted the set and gave Terry the thumbs up. He walked away as he continued to chew. Terry couldn't look at Char because he'd start laughing. He bit his lip before starting.

"Space Adventurer Terry to Leader X, over," Terry said.

Nathan's face appeared on the comm screen. "Are we using code now?" Nathan asked tiredly.

"Sorry, Nathan. There's a lull in the fighting, and maybe we're a little punchy. No Bad Company casualties. Resupply is complete. We have a Podder with us, but he's a good one. We're now in the area of the bad Podders, but we've found the Crenellians, even rescued one from the blue Podders, and don't ask. That's what the good stalk-heads call the bad stalk-heads. I'm sorry to say that the Crenellians seem to be bad, too. I'm not sure there's anyone on this planet I like besides the people we brought."

"Do you have an idea when you'll be able to wrap things up?" Nathan asked.

"I do not, but we have a better strategic plan now. We're going to roll up the Crenellians until we find their head shed, then we're going to drag their dumb asses into a meet and greet with their enemy. We'll hurt as many of them as we have to until we find someone who will talk. We have eight mechs now and with a full resupply, we can mow down both sides like we're a harvester clearing a wheat field, but I won't do that, Nathan. I didn't sign up for genocide."

"I would never ask that of you, TH. Genocide doesn't help the Federation, doesn't help anyone. We need these two to be at peace and then become contributing members of the Federation. They're in the buffer zone. The more buffer zone systems we can bring into the fold, the better protected the entire Federation will be. Your job is to make sure no one commits genocide. A happy, loyal, and trustworthy system. That's what we're looking for."

"Happy? Did I mention that there's a civil war down here? The Podders live underground, so that's why the Crenellians didn't know, or they didn't care to learn. They put themselves right in the middle of it. The group they negotiated the contract with wasn't the one who occupied the area where they started their mining process. That was the first group's way to use the Crenellians against their enemies. It was a three-way dick job. Once we shed light on that, I think we'll be able to end this thing. The biggest obstacle is the civil war, but I have a plan…" Terry turned to Char and winked.

She looked skeptical.

"I'm sure you do. Let me know when you're able to wrap things up and whatever you do, don't kill any of the Crenellians. Their checks may be hard to cash after that."

"They write checks?" Terry blurted.

"Well…" Nathan ran a hand through his hair. "They don't, but you know what I mean. We trade in gold and rare minerals."

"One last thing, Nathan." Terry mirrored the head of the Bad Company's gesture by removing his helmet and running his hand through his hair. "Christina is doing great. She helped protect the weretigers when they got into a scrape. I'm happy to have her on board and proud of what she's done."

"I'm happy to hear you say that. I'll let Ecaterina know. She'll be relieved, because of course, we worry. What kind of parents would we be if we didn't? Anything else?"

"That's it for now, Nathan. Walton out." Before the signal could close, multiple railguns barked, and the sound crashed through the confined space of the cavern. Two mechs opened up and the beastly railguns they carried sent a stream of death into the tunnels.

"They're coming," Kaeden said, using his suit's external speakers.

THE EMPIRE'S RESEARCH **& Development asteroids, affectionately called R2D2**

Ted looked at the researchers from Team BMW. No one looked spectacular. Bobcat, Marcus, and Tina were talking about a new beer recipe. Ted didn't have anything to add since he never bothered while Terry Henry was brewing his draughts.

"Hey, Ted!" Tina called, turning and walking toward him. "We heard Terry Henry spent decades working on brewing beer without using hops. What did he come up with?"

Ted shrugged, but the woman was approaching and wanted an answer. "I don't know. I don't like beer." He expected his answer would suffice.

It didn't. "You what?" she asked in a low voice, before speaking over her shoulder. "Hey, guys, Ted doesn't like beer." She turned back to the werewolf. "What do you like?"

"Engineering," Ted replied without hesitation. "Engineering challenges, most of all."

"Aren't you married? Didn't I see that beautiful wife of yours? How did you manage that if your two top things are engineering?" Bobcat asked, joining the conversation.

"She begged me to marry her, so we came to a mutually beneficial arrangement," Ted tried to explain.

"You what?" Tina wondered. "How does that work?"

"Her husband died during a Forsaken attack, mainly from old age. She didn't want to go through that again and I was the only one available. She makes sure I eat," Ted said matter-of-factly.

"She makes sure you eat? That's *all* you get from being

married to an ultra-hottie like her?" Bobcat pursed his lips and raised his eyebrows, curious about Ted's reply.

Ted pulled at the collar of his ship suit, suddenly feeling hot and constricted. He could feel his face flush.

"Tell me you have kids," Tina pressed.

"Yes," Ted admitted. "We have three, but they're back on Earth."

Ted wondered why he was getting interrogated. He replayed the conversation in his mind, trying to follow the logic. In the end, he determined that next time, if someone asked, he would tell them that he liked beer.

"Thank goodness," Bobcat said, looking at Tina. "I thought you were a geek like us, but you're a family man at heart, enjoying regular meals of muff pie and furburger."

Ted didn't know what that meant, but decided that he wanted the conversation to end. "Yes, all of that and more," he offered, just so he could continue on a different topic. "What project will I work on? I hope it's the miniaturization of the gate drive technology. Is that what it is? I hope that's it!"

Marcus, Tina, and Bobcat looked at each other. "All that and more, huh?" Bobcat wondered, and then conceded that Ted could have been a dynamo when the lights were off.

Marcus stepped in. "Miniaturization of the gate drive? We already have that, but the issues there are that it is prohibitively expensive and the EI or the AI has to commit suicide if the ship is compromised. If we can fix both those issues, think of how small we could make the universe."

"But the universe is constantly expanding," Ted replied.

"Expanding where, Ted? There can only be one

constant and that's infinity, don't you agree?" Tina suggested.

Ted looked at Tina but didn't see the woman. He was lost in thought, trying to answer the question that had no answer. Not without more data.

"And next time," Bobcat started, putting a friendly hand on Ted's shoulder. "Be more familiar with beer since that is the universe's number one priority. Some would say the secret to life, the universe, and everything is forty-two, but the right answer is beer."

PODDERN

Marcie stood with her hands on her hips, staring at the man. To his credit, he held her gaze.

"I asked what you did. You can tell me or I start breaking fingers. Or—" She looked at the weretigers. "—I could let them eat you. You'll see bits of your body disappear into their mouths until you pass out from the pain. Then, they'll finish you off. You're barely more than a snack, so they'll start on him next."

Marcie pointed with her thumb to the man at the next station.

"I'll tell you what I do," the third Crenellian said softly. "I don't wish to see any of the others injured."

"Now we're getting somewhere. Please trust me when I say that I don't want to hurt anyone. We're here at the request of the Crenellian president to end this war. We don't let our clients dictate how that happens, so you need to help us understand the strategic and tactical situations. I think you're going to find out that we want the same thing you do—finish this and go home."

The third man down didn't nod, he only looked at Marcie with his big eyes. The weretigers watched him while Christina continued to straddle the first man, drool dripping on his face with clock-like regularity.

"I understand. I would like to go home. I've been here from the start, just like almost everyone here."

15

Kae gritted his teeth and growled as he fired his railgun into the mass of blue bodies. "Would you fucking stop!" he howled through his suit's speakers. His order echoed with the cracks from the railgun.

His cry fell on deaf ears. They kept coming, wading through a deeper and deeper mass of blue goo, the remains of those who went before. Kelly stood beside him, firing regularly into the bodies. Slugs pinged continuously off the armored suits. The blue Podders marched ahead, relentlessly, until the wall of dead blocked those behind.

Joseph leaned on the Bundin's shell, talking quickly.

Timmons, Sue, Shonna, and Merrit stood behind two mechs in another tunnel, picking Podders one at a time as they appeared. There was only one blue wave assault, but the Podders underestimated the human defense. The aliens couldn't draw all the forces away, letting them sneak past. There were no gaps.

"Joseph?" Terry asked as his eyes jumped from one

tunnel to the next, gauging the level of the attack, trying to determine if he was missing something, or if it was what it looked like—Podders throwing their lives away.

"He says lead with lights!" Joseph yelled over the cacophony of railguns and slug-throwers.

Activate your suit's lights, Terry told the company. Only those wearing the powered suits responded. The lights came on, then blared into the darkness.

What's up, Dad? Kae asked.

Recommendation from Bundin. It has to be better than mowing them down.

I'm willing to try anything else. This isn't fun and there's no honor in this, Kae replied.

We can be mercenaries, but I don't want to ever act like mercenaries. We will always stay true to ourselves, Terry said.

The railguns stopped firing.

They're retreating, Kaeden finally reported.

"Report!" Terry yelled into the cavern.

"No penetration of the line. None of the Podders made it this far," Kimber stated.

Timmons walked from one person to the next. His team was unscathed. He waved at Terry. "Nothing to report here."

Ramses, Auburn, and Cory stood behind the canister, watching the others, ready to help where needed when called.

"Prep a reload for Kae and Kelly," Terry told Auburn. The eight mechs shined the full power of their lights into the tunnels.

"Since they can operate above ground, I doubt the lights will hold them off for long. Is there anything else our friend can tell us to help us to *not* kill these people?" Terry asked.

Joseph and Bundin communicated for a while, before the vampire turned away. "Nothing, TH," Joseph said, his head hanging. He said you're going to have to kill a lot more of them if you want to make an impression."

Terry stepped through the rocks and rubble to stand next to the Podder.

"I want to prove you wrong, that we can do this without washing this world in the Podders' blue blood."

THE *WAR AXE*

The situation stabilized enough that Micky was able to sit down and think through what he wanted to do next.

"Open the comm channel to Colonel Walton, Smedley," the captain said as he leaned back and draped his legs over the desk.

"Of course. Standby," the EI replied.

The screen on the wall came to life, showing an image filled with static and an inset of Micky. He waited as the company on Tissikinnon Four set up their system. Terry's face appeared.

"Micky!" he said in a big voice. "You caught us during a lull in the fighting. Thanks for the extra suits. They came in handy. The Podders don't have a chance against them."

Terry grimaced at the last statement. Micky understood.

"I'm glad everything arrived intact. Is there any way you can find out how in the holy hell a planet like this has weapons of the sort that they used on us during our last run?"

"Explain that more, if you would, Skipper. Did you get hit during the run?" Concern clouded Terry's face.

Micky went into more detail than Terry wanted to hear, but the colonel listened politely.

"A cloud of mines that miraculously appeared in your flight path after you juked to avoid being predictable. Pure dumb luck?" Terry waved his hand at the screen. "I don't believe in luck like that, and I suspect you don't either. Looking at how the Podders operate, that couldn't be them. There's no way they have space travel, even. My guess is that they paid someone, which means there is yet another player in the middle of this mess."

"Could be," the captain conceded as he pursed his lips and thought through the options. "Are we sure it wasn't the Crenellians?"

"What would they gain by attacking the people they hired?" Terry wondered. "We'll have to ask our favorite aliens all these questions and more. If it turns out that it was the Crenellians, then I will burn the president's palace down, with him in it."

Micky nodded approvingly. "And I'll help."

PODDERN

"We came here in peace, having traded technology for mining rights. We bored a few test shafts, backfilled the ones that didn't work, and for reference, after we were done, you couldn't tell there was ever a shaft there," the Crenellian added proudly.

Marcie rolled her finger, suggesting the alien continue. He looked at her motion oddly.

"Continue," she said, having quickly learned that the Crenellians didn't have the same gestures as humans.

"Well, the Tiskers found fault and reneged on the deal. We figured that out when they killed the mining crew. All of them."

"Tell me something I don't know," Marcie cautioned.

The man stood and walked up to Marcie. She was unconcerned as the alien was unarmed. He stopped in front of her and leaned his head back to look up at her. "The technology that we traded for the mining rights was advanced weaponry, some artillery, but mainly, an advanced planetary defense system. Of course, we have a back-door code, but everything else is in the control of the natives."

"Now that's something I didn't know and is very interesting," Marcie contemplated calling her father-in-law, but wanted more to tell him. "What are you doing in here? This looks like a control room, so it begs the question, what are you controlling."

She looked at the collected group. They were all looking at her, none of them blinking. She couldn't read their body language and had no idea if they were angry, happy, tired, nervous, or something else in entirety.

"We are running a remote force to attack the flank of the Tisker army," the small alien said.

"Where are your soldiers?" Marcie asked.

"We don't have anyone of such low class. We built the machines to do that for us, just like mining."

Marcie thought for a moment. She needed more time.

"Pause everything. Stand down the attack while we wait for the colonel. He needs to hear what you have to say."

"That is out of the question. It took us the past two months to build the program for this offensive. It is set on automatic at this point. There's no stopping it."

"Fuck that. If you can program it to do something, it's easy to tell it to stop. Stop the attack," Marcie ordered.

None of the Crenellians moved. Marcie swung her railgun to the front and aimed at one of the workstations. She counted down from the three to zero, but the aliens didn't budge.

The railgun cracked and the workstation exploded into a rain of debris that peppered the wall. The Crenellian who had been standing in front of her dropped to the floor and covered his head.

She aimed at the next workstation. The Crenellian hurriedly got up from his seat and jumped aside. She counted down again. At zero, the railgun dart pulverized a second workstation.

After the third workstation was destroyed, the alien on the floor before her turned his head and looked up. "There may be a way," he offered.

"JOSEPH?" Terry prodded again, but the vampire was deeply engaged in a conversation with the Podder.

Char tapped Terry on the shoulder. "Bugging him every two seconds isn't going to get you what you want."

"What do I want?" Terry asked, unhappy with how long

it was taking Joseph in a conversation that Terry had no idea about the topic.

"You want to know where the leaders are so you can storm up to them and tell them how it's going to be." She turned her head as he scowled.

"Okay, that is what I want, but why is it taking so long?"

"If I could answer that, then we would already be on our way to knock some sense into these creatures."

Terry's expression softened, and then he chuckled. "Petricia?" he asked when he saw her watching him.

"I'm with Char. Nothing would make me happier than seeing the end of this bloodbath and be back on board the *War Axe* on our way home," Petricia replied.

"Keeg Station. Our home," Terry replied. "I like ground beneath my feet, air that hasn't been recycled and processed, the waves of an ocean lapping at the beach. We need a planet with all that for our secret lair. We can call it Our Secret Lair."

"Lair?" Char looked at him. "I suppose you're still angry that I didn't want to go to Lake Geneva all those years ago."

"A little. Come on, Char, GaryCon! I missed it and you wouldn't even let me go pay homage. And lair is a great word!" Terry tipped his head back and puffed out his chest.

Everyone who could see was watching. The throwdowns between Terry Henry Walton and Charumati were the stuff of legends. Few had seen the real deal firsthand, but the stories were passed from one to another as if gospel.

"Since when do you not do something you want to do?" Char reached out one finger and drew a line along Terry's cheek, trailing down his neck where she lightly touched his skin.

Goosebumps popped out on his arm. He looked around and found all eyes on him. He leaned close, eyes dilated as his blood rushed to his head. "Are you using sex to manipulate me?" he asked.

She raised one eyebrow, and her purple eyes sparkled in the semi-darkness.

"Again," he added.

"Have you been in touch with Marcie lately?" Char asked.

"Your evil plot to distract me has killed two minutes that may have otherwise been spent stomping around impatiently. I thank you, my lover."

"Any time, my big husky hunk of man candy," Char replied.

Cordelia walked up to them. "Are you two done making a spectacle?" she asked.

Terry adjusted his helmet as he looked thoughtfully at his daughter. Dokken was at Cory's side, her hand resting on his head.

"You little turncoat," Terry told him. He cocked his head back and forth as he looked at the colonel.

Marcie, do you have anything new? Terry asked using his comm chip.

TH, I was just going to call. These knuckleheads are fighting this war remotely. They don't have any soldiers, only technicians and computers. All the hardware we've been facing is of Crenellian manufacture. They sold it to the Podders. I am in the process of convincing these little bastards that they need to stop this attack that's about to kick off. I'll check in as soon as we've come to an agreement.

"That's different," Terry said aloud after Marcie signed off. "Gimme comm, Auburn. I need to talk with Micky, ASAP."

MICKY SAT in the captain's chair. He didn't see the bridge crew or the screens showing the immensity of space before them. He only saw the damage reports scrolling across his screens.

The Pod Doc had done its job, and the injured crewman was better and back at work with the hull repair crew.

The hangar bay door still wouldn't open, but Blagun had not reported any changes to his original repair time-line, which said that he needed two more days to get one door operational.

Terry's face appeared on Micky's screen. "Thanks for the warning, Smedley," Micky grumbled before turning on the charm. "Why, Terry Henry, calling me back so soon?"

"I wanted to let you know that the weaponry in orbit is of Crenellian manufacture. They sold it to the Podders as part of the mining contract," Terry said.

"So the *War Axe* got pummeled by gear from the people who hired us, but they failed to tell us that we would be fighting their equipment. I am not pleased by this." Micky clenched his jaw.

"That is an understatement," Terry said. "You want to let Nathan know? I feel like we're going to be moving pretty soon and I need to get ready. Walton out."

Micky watched his screen go blank. "Smedley, please connect me with Nathan Lowell."

PODDERN

Terry watched Auburn put the comm gear away, almost feeling guilty for lying to Micky San Marino. Terry didn't want to call Nathan because he was spitting mad. He didn't want to talk with the boss while he was that angry.

Call it professional pride.

Marcie, I'm on my way over there. I'll have Dokken track the weretigers. Is there any tricks to finding you? Terry asked.

None. I'll let the door guards know that you're on your way, Marcie replied.

"Fancy a walk?" Terry asked Char.

"With you?" she said. "Always."

"Come on, Dokken, we've got some cats to track. You, too, and bring him." Terry nodded toward Ramses, Auburn, Cory, and the freed Crenellian. "Kimber! Hold the fort. You're in charge until we get back."

"Yes, sir," Kimber replied, immediately heading for Timmons to get his help with the Etheric.

"Joseph, keep working with Bundin and see what other surprises we can find in the minefield that is Tissikinnon Four."

16

"You're in deep shit now," Marcie told the aliens. "Christina. It's about time you let him up."

Christina stepped back, and the alien got to his feet, furiously wiping at his face. The werewolf chuckled.

The weretigers paced. The two warriors were relaxed with their weapons aimed at the aliens. Marcie stood in the middle of them, glaring from face to face.

"I answered honestly. You should leave. We have a mess to clean up and work to do," the cooperative alien told her.

"And you said there may be a way to stop your attack. Spill it, buddy."

"Spill what?" the alien asked.

"Just tell me, no, better yet, tell me as you are making it happen." Marcie loomed over the small alien.

The Crenellian moved to an open terminal, one that had not yet been destroyed, and started tapping buttons. "There."

"There, what? The attack is stopped?"

"Temporarily, yes. All units are actively engaged in solar charging. When they hit one hundred percent, they'll resume the attack."

"That doesn't work for me, you little fuck," Marcie told him. "Think harder and halt the attack."

"Once the attack is launched, nearly all commands are locked out. We have no control. The units will fight, mercilessly, until victory has been achieved."

"How do you define victory?" Marcie asked.

"The complete and unconditional surrender of the enemy!" the alien declared.

"Fine. Tell your units that the Podders have surrendered unconditionally and that you need them to stand the fuck down." The logic made sense to Marcie.

The Crenellian asked the leader of the group. The second alien replied. The two engaged in a short conversation. The first one returned to the computer terminal and started mashing buttons.

Marcie watched, knowing that she wouldn't understand if he was giving the attack units the command to stand down or destroy the planet.

"When they wake up from recharging," the alien started, "they will receive the updated information that the enemy has surrendered."

"And then what?" Marcie asked, unsure that the alien was being completely honest.

"The units will check. If they find any Tiskers with weapons, they will attack and destroy them. We have a saying on the Crenellian home world—trust but verify. It is instrumental in all our programming."

"The Podders haven't surrendered, so you've actually accomplished nothing," Marcie snarled, reaching for the man. "I ought to wring your neck."

The alien stood his ground. Marcie stopped herself, because they didn't seem to respond to physical threats. The only action that received a response was the destruction of the equipment, and that was only marginally successful.

"Who's in charge of this mob?" Marcie asked.

"He is," the man said, pointing to the Crenellian who finished wiping werewolf drool off his bald head.

Marcie grabbed the leader. "What's your name?" she demanded.

"Tik'Po'Rout," he said without inflection, standing up straight. The top of his head was even with Marcie's chest. He looked at her ballistic vest where Podder slugs had impacted. She let him study the damage. He reached out a hand to examine the material. "What is this vest made of?"

"I don't know. Kevlar maybe?" Marcie didn't expect they knew what Kevlar was.

"Is there any way we could get a sample of this?" he asked.

"I don't think so. We need to wear these, thanks to you spinning up the natives."

"Spinning the natives? Can you imagine that?" he asked his fellow Crenellians. "Us. In the amusement ride industry."

The aliens shook as if shivering.

"That is why he is the leader. He sees the bright side of every situation," the first alien said.

The warriors looked at each other and chuckled.

169

Marcie joined them. The aliens stopped shivering. Their facial expressions never changed throughout.

A greeting and a short exchange at the entrance to the underground signaled Colonel Terry Henry Walton's arrival.

"WHAT DO YOU THINK, KEL?" Kaeden asked over the suit-to-suit communication.

"I think I love this suit," she replied quickly. "Will I get to keep it?"

"Judging from what we've run into down here, I think the mech unit has arrived. We will always need this kind of heavy firepower," Kaeden said as he reviewed the status indicators on his HUD.

Kelly sidestepped and then raised up on her tippy toes, lifting an armored hand to the ceiling. She scraped out a small section and then held it in her hand. "Sixty-four percent granite, silica, traces of gold... Did you know it could do this?"

Kae turned his head to look at the other armored warrior. He could have skewed the HUD to look anywhere as the suit had eyes in the back of its head, but Kaeden found it disconcerting to see one image while looking in a different direction. Maybe in the future, they'd call him old-school for doing it that way.

"Do what?" he asked.

"It analyzes whatever is inside the glove."

"Holy shit!" Kae had studied the suit exhaustively, but

only as it related to combat. He scraped some stone off the wall and held it in his hand. Nothing happened.

"You have to crunch it up and hold it in your closed fist," Kelly advised.

Kae ground the rocks to dust using the suit's power. A small window appeared in his HUD that started listing the elements within the sample.

"This is really cool," he added. A red light started blinking before his face. "Dammit!"

Low power.

"What's wrong?" Kelly asked.

"I need to go topside and recharge," Kae answered.

"Why don't you use the power supply that arrived in the canister?"

"They sent the recharging unit? I love those guys!"

DOKKEN WAS FIRST DOWN the tunnel and ran into the room that had been carved from the rock of Tissikinnon Four. When he saw the weretigers, his lip quivered as he wanted to growl at them. He knew they were Aaron and Yanmei, but they were also friends of his arch enemy. He swung wide, rubbing his body against Christina as he passed, and stopped by Marcie, wagging his tail.

Terry appeared and waved, then looked at the Crenellians. Marcie pointed to the one in charge. Terry approached and took a knee so he could look eye to eye with the alien.

"Your bullshit in orbit scratched the paint on my new

ride. I'll need you to shut that all down so when the *Axe* returns, they don't have to play mumbly peg."

Marcie shook her head, motioning for Terry to stop. He looked up to her. "They are very literal. This one's name is Tik'Po'Rout," she advised.

Terry nodded and looked back to the Crenellian.

"Tik'Po'Rout. Please disable the orbital security system. Right now would be good. And any of your remote combat systems down here, disable them too," Terry said, ice dripping from his words.

Char joined them, then Ramses, Cory, and Auburn. Auburn was carrying the Crenellian who had no chance of keeping up with the enhanced group as they ran from the cavern to the outpost.

Two of the aliens who had not spoken hurried to meet Auburn and help their fellow. His mood changed entirely as they held his hands and led him to a seat.

Marcie watched closely, and Terry watched, too. The sum total of his experience with the aliens was lugging the nearly catatonic Crenellian around. He vowed to study the alien cultures more before conducting future interdictions. His assumption that they would figure it out was costing the company time and resources. The cultures were so different that projecting humanity's strengths and weaknesses onto them was counterproductive.

Char saw Terry struggling with his perceptions of the aliens. He wanted to hate them because of the president's seeming duplicity. But the humanity that they were showing for their fellow suggested that they deserved consideration at a different level.

She knelt next to TH, her purple eyes sparkling. The alien leader reached out a hand and touched the silver streak of hair that trailed down one side of her face.

"Why is this silver and the rest brown?" he asked.

"It's my belly fur. You see, I'm a werewolf, like her." Char pointed to Christina.

Tik'Po'Rout's eyes followed where she was pointing and rested on the werewolf. He turned back to Char.

"Like her, but not like her."

Marcie wondered where the alien had gotten his insight, because he was spot on. She looked at Terry and he looked back to his daughter-in-law. They both nodded slightly.

"Exactly," Char replied. "We want to end this war for two reasons. First, we were hired to end it by your president. Second, we've had about enough of Poddern. You can help us, which in turn, helps you. Tell us what we need to know to finish this war."

"Then let us continue our attacks for the final solution," the alien said firmly.

Char closed her eyes and controlled her breathing. Terry's nostrils flared.

"That's not going to work for us. The people of this planet are the best ones to determine what they can share with the universe," Char said in a low voice. "The Federation can't support genocide or plundering a planet of its natural resources. It simply won't work, so the solution that we must arrive at will involve as many people as possible surviving, people on both sides of this war."

Terry clenched his teeth so hard that his face vibrated.

"We had a contract, and they broke it. There must be repercussions," the alien countered.

"There have already been repercussions. How many Podders have died in this war?"

"I don't have an accurate count."

"Guess," Terry growled.

"We don't like to guess."

"Do it for me. I won't tell. Ten thousand? Twenty thousand?" Terry prodded.

The alien hesitated before looking to his fellows. Terry and Char couldn't tell if any of the humanoids moved, but finally the leader conceded. "More like a million."

Terry's heart sank. The Bad Company had done their share of damage, but nothing on the scale of the Crenellians and their automated war machines.

"Tell us where this force is that will be conducting the attack. We can wait no longer," Terry insisted.

The first alien who had helped accessed the screen behind him and pulled up a map. He pointed. Terry and Marcie studied it while Char stared at Tik'Po'Rout.

Kaeden, I need you to take your mechs southwest from the cave-in. There's an automated Crenellian force that will be attacking the Podders shortly. This weaponry must be obliterated. If it takes every rocket your mechs have, do it, Terry ordered.

On our way, came Kae's simple reply.

"Where is the main Crenellian headquarters?" Terry asked.

None of the Crenellians spoke.

"Auburn, set up the comm and let's see if Smedley can get into their system." Terry motioned to the warriors. "Get them out of here."

With a snarl from the weretigers, a growl from the werewolf, and helping hands from the Bad Company, the aliens were removed from their outpost.

"My president will hear about this!" the alien leader cried.

"Yes, he will, and he'll hear it from me," Terry called after them. He looked at Char. "Are you thinking what I'm thinking?"

"That you miss the days when the enemy was evil Forsaken who trembled at the sound of your name?" she offered.

"Your radar must be off. I was wondering if these guys are the galaxy's douchebags. I want to put my fist through their smug little dickheads."

"I guess I was thinking that, too."

"Good effort trying to play nice, but I don't think these guys have much control. I see this group as a bunch of ultra-loyal programmers. We have yet to meet the knucklehead in charge," Terry said.

Auburn gave the thumbs up.

"Smedley, my man, what's the haps?"

"I'm sorry, Colonel Walton, has your brain been injured?" Smedley replied through the communication system's speakers.

"No, I'm fine. We have the Crenellians' computers in this outpost and was hoping that you'd be able to tap into them, learn some stuff, like where the headquarters might be, the access codes to shut down the planetary defense software. If that doesn't work, we're going to have to incrementally destroy every piece of the Crenellian war machine, no matter who is operating it, the dickheads or the stalk-heads."

Char elbowed Terry in the ribs, hitting him below the edge of his ballistic vest. "I mean the Crenellians or the Podders," he corrected himself, while picking up the comm panel and pointing it around the space.

"Punch some of the keys and let's see if we can see what kind of digital footprint this thing leaves."

Terry complied. Then started punching specific buttons at Smedley's request. The others left to go outside. Marcie remained behind with Auburn to search the space. There were a couple doors that they had not opened.

"THE CRENELLIANS SOLD the hardware to the Podders that caused a great deal of damage to the *War Axe*," Micky started explaining as soon as he saw Nathan's face.

Nathan Lowell took a long, slow drink of Pepsi. He closed his eyes and smacked his lips when he finished.

"Sounds like a system that we could put around Keeg Station, as well as some of our other high-value planets. Can you get the tech details for us?"

Micky twisted his mouth around. He wanted Nathan to be angry, not look at the damage to the *War Axe* as a technology demonstration. He could see the cold logic, but he wanted to be angry. He snorted as he understood why TH didn't want to call.

"I don't know. Terry is on the planet right now, and I think they're discussing the meaning of life with the Crenellians they've found."

"He knows not to kill any of them, right?" Nathan said, suddenly concerned.

Micky shrugged. "Smedley, can you tie us in with Colonel Walton, please?"

"I have him online already, let me patch him in," Smedley replied. A split image appeared on Micky's screen with Nathan on the left and Terry on the right. Terry was poking at a screen.

"I'm hitting the fucking button, you half-baked ass monkey! These stupid symbols on the screen aren't doing anything. Come on, fucker!"

"Terry?" Micky asked.

"Oh, hey! There you are," Terry said, wiping his hand off on his pants leg. "I'll get you for this, Smedley."

"Where are the Crenellians?" Nathan asked.

"We took them outside while we tried to patch Smedley into their system. We're still working on that."

"I gathered," Nathan replied.

"I *am* pushing the one on the right. No, my other right. Fucking Smedley!" Terry continued his monologue, then looked up in surprise. "Smedley's in."

Terry Henry turned to face the communication system, listening intently as Nathan started to speak.

"We could use that orbital defensive system the Crenellians sold the Podders, and anything else they have. Try to get schematics and programming for all of it, TH." Nathan had leaned forward and was looking intently at the screen.

"I understand, Nathan. I think we can leverage this mission into something far more than a few bars of gold. If we have those weapon systems, then we'll be better equipped the next time we run across them. I doubt

Poddern is the only planet they've been sold to," Terry said before he looked over his shoulder and saw the screen scrolling and flashing as Smedley tore through the Crenellian programming.

"What's your status, Micky?" Nathan asked.

"The worst of it is we lost our main weapon on the starboard side. We can't open our hangar bay doors, but we didn't lose anyone. All personal injuries have been fixed by the Pod Doc. Structural repairs continue," the captain reported.

"You can't open the hangar bay doors?" Terry said, seeing his mission getting extended because the *War Axe* couldn't recover the drop ships.

"Not yet, TH. The doors are our number one priority. Commander Lagunov assures me that we'll be able to recover you and your people whenever you call for pickup. You're not calling for pickup right now, are you?"

"Micky! That's a good one, but no. Not yet. Once Smedley finds us the Crenellian headquarters, then we'll be able to move this along a little more smartly. I suspect we'll be using all our rockets shortly and may need another resupply, though, if we're to take on more of these roaming automated combat units."

"We can't resupply you for a few days. We have one more canister partially finished, but all resources have been allocated to ship repair. As long as that defensive system is still in place, a return high-speed pass could be problematic," Micky replied.

Terry pursed his lips before answering. "We'll make do. Fix our ride, because the next time you come back, it'll be to pick us up. We'll figure this out, won't we, Smedley?"

Nathan and Micky watched as Terry turned back to the monitor and Smedley's work with the system. From off-screen, the men heard Marcie's voice. "Hey, Terry! We found something."

17

Poddern

Kaeden's armored unit ran at a ground-eating pace, jogging in the daylight, which allowed them to recharge more power than they were using.

Capples was bringing up the rear and carrying the power supply. It was large enough that he had to use two hands and run with an ambling gait. He held it in front of him, using the suit's sensors slaved to the others in the unit to make sure he knew where he was stepping.

The delay in not being able to run at max speed was worth it, in Kae's mind, because he had almost redlined his power when he received the colonel's call to arms.

The last thing he needed was to spend another long night on the ground outside of a dead suit.

Kae waved his arms, signaling the unit to spread out. He had the point, Capples was directly behind him while three each spread out to the sides. They all saw the unit up ahead. Kae raised his hand, palm forward to slow down.

They walked while their eyes, suit sensors, and micro-drones collected information on their target.

"Holy shit," Kaeden whispered as it came into focus.

A massive tank, the size of a small spaceship, sat unmoving. It bristled with weaponry, missiles, gun tubes, radars, and other protrusions. The size of a football field or a soccer pitch, it sat and dominated the landscape.

"Ideas?" Kae asked.

"Not sure our rockets will do anything to that beast," Cantor suggested.

"The Beast. How in the fuck did they get it here?" Praeter asked.

Kae shrugged and started walking toward it. An energy beam plowed the earth in front of him. "RUN!" he yelled.

He didn't mean from it. He meant to it, and that was how the warriors responded.

Capples dropped the power supply and spooled up two rockets as he zigzagged slowly, building the distance between him and Kaeden.

The others spread out and accelerated, jigging erratically as they ran. The Beast's weapon systems fired repeatedly, but the targeting couldn't keep up with the mechs.

Kae led the way and leapt as high as the suit would take him. He contemplated using the jets to boost his height, but decided against it. He didn't want to fly over the tank. He wanted to land in the middle of it.

An energy beam grazed the suit. He could feel the heat, briefly, and then it was gone. Two red lights appeared, flashed twice, and turned back to green by the time he landed. Once on the tank, he crouched and looked for a target, but found that he had time. The tank's weapons were aimed outboard or upward. The designers hadn't contemplated an attack like the one that the Bad Company had just made.

One by one, the others vaulted to the top of The Beast. They cheered for Capples as he brought up the rear. Once the others were safe, he accelerated and jumped. A beam weapon hit him square in the chest and threw him back to the ground.

Kaeden didn't hesitate. He scrambled to get off the tank and staying low, ran to his teammate. He picked him up and threw him over one shoulder, then ran back to the tank. Beam weapons pocked the ground around him.

Railguns opened up, destroying each of the weapons that fired. One by one, they fell silent. Kae took three last steps and jumped, landing on the back of the tank. He walked up the glacis until he was on the vehicle's flat back, where he laid Capples on it. Kae could see through the visor that the man was alive and groaning.

"Talk to me, Cap," Kaeden encouraged.

"Singed...around the edges...slammed around...just like in training," the man managed to say.

Kae helped him to a sitting position and propped him against a bulbous projection. "Hold the fort. We're going to see if we can get inside and find the off switch."

MARCIE POINTED into the space behind the control room. "What do you think of that?" she asked.

"Is that what I think it is?" Terry wondered.

Auburn went inside, before quickly returning. "It is, but

not for us. Who would have thought they would build an executive bathroom for this small crew? Showers, hot tub, sauna, sweet soft-seat toilets. Too bad everything is child-sized. The showerhead comes to my waist."

"So close. It would have been nice to cycle everyone through the showers. Oh well, they'll just have to wait until they get back on board the ship." Terry looked forlornly at the bathroom that was grossly out of place as part of an expeditionary warfighting outpost. "Maybe the Crenellians are more cultured than we gave them credit for. Anyone who builds this—" Terry pointed into the bathroom. "—to support this—" He pointed into the control room. "—has their priorities in the right place. If they only had a coffee maker…"

Marcie opened the door to the next room.

Terry peeked around the corner. There was no coffee, but he saw a well-stocked kitchen. He couldn't recognize any of the foods and didn't bother sampling them. The third and final room was austere, consisting of four bunkbeds and gray walls.

"A kitchen, a styling bathroom, and all the rest is work chic." Terry shook his head. "Smedley!"

"Yes, Colonel Walton. I am always on the edge of my seat as I await your bellowed summons."

Marcie and Auburn snickered.

"What did you find out?" Terry asked, confident that Smedley's evolution to becoming sentient was nearly complete. Terry wondered why the target of the EI's humor always seemed to be the colonel himself.

"I have everything I could recover downloaded and am analyzing now. I have to replicate a few of their interfaces so the data makes sense. Imagine pulling a graphics file up in a reading program. It doesn't work unless the program knows the file type. It shouldn't be long. I expect to have a full analysis within a day," Smedley replied.

"Sounds great, Smedley, but a day isn't going to work for me. I want to get off this rock now, but I can't do that as long as there's still a war. To end the war, I need you to tell me where the Crenellian headquarters is."

"I have that information. Let me display it for you." A map appeared on the screen that they'd been using.

"Son of a bitch," Terry grumbled. "How far away is that?"

"One thousand, four hundred kilometers."

"We'll use the drop ships," Terry replied definitively. "Thanks, Smedley. One more thing. What kind of defenses do they have protecting it?"

"That is what will take another day or so. I will call you sooner if I have it."

Terry nodded and closed the comm channel. He quickly packed the gear. He thought he heard the water running in the bathroom. When he checked, he found Marcie washing her hair.

"Since I was here and you were still on the phone." She pulled a neatly folded towel from the stack and dried her mid-length blonde hair before bunching it back under her helmet. "I feel like a new woman."

"I'm sure Kaeden will appreciate your efforts. Have you heard from him?"

"FIRE IN THE HOLE!" Kae yelled as he slammed a grenade through a small hatch he'd been able to pry open. He stood on the hatch to hold it closed in case anyone tried to escape.

The explosion bounced him into the air. When his feet hit the tank, he ripped the hatch open and shined a light inside. Unless he left his armored suit behind, there was no chance of getting inside. Even with his suit off, he wasn't sure he'd fit.

"Fleeter. Kelly. You're the two smallest. I need one of you to ditch your suit and climb inside this thing, see if you can find a way to shut it down. I'd go, but I won't fit."

"I'll do it," Fleeter said softly. "What the hell. No guts, no glory."

She walked across the top of the tank to join Kae outside the hatch. Fleeter parked her suit, the back opened, and she climbed out. She stretched in the open air, before catching herself and looking around.

"First time out of the suit?" Kae asked.

She thought for a moment before answering. "Yes."

"Disconcerting, isn't it? One second, you're indestructible, and then you're bare-ass naked before the world, the epitome of vulnerability."

She had her clothes on, but understood what he was saying.

"Exactly that," she replied, while still crouching close to her suit. "It's really loud out here."

Kae had set the suit to share sounds that he thought he needed to hear. He changed the filter setting to ambient. "Holy crap! Is that an engine spinning up?"

The tank lurched and Kae almost lost his balance.

Fleeter grabbed her suit to keep from falling. "Get in there and shut this thing down. Here, take a couple motivators with you." Kae handed her two grenades.

She didn't take them as she held up a single finger. *Wait one.*

Fleeter climbed through the hatch, finding it a tight squeeze until she was through, then she could see narrow and low passageways. One going forward and aft, while one headed to the other side of the massive vehicle.

"Grenades!" she yelled through the open hatch, and Kae handed them down. She hooked them over her belt. She pulled her combat knife. The mech's railgun was too large for her to carry. She looked at it hanging from her parked armor, and then looked back to Kaeden. "See you on the flipside, boss."

He gave her the thumbs up. The other mechs started firing their railguns. Kaeden rushed away to find out what was happening.

"HE WON'T ANSWER," Marcie said, looking confused.

"Get our friend back in here so he can tell us what's going on out there. Has their remote weapon system engaged?"

"Get the other Crenellian back in here!" Marcie yelled down the tunnel.

"I could have done that," Terry said as he watched Auburn pack and stow the comm gear.

Terry stroked his chin and started to pace. Marcie let him go. Dokken and Christina were with the alien. He looked at the screens and back to Marcie. He didn't say anything.

"Please pull up the status of the weapon system that you turned loose. We want to know if it has engaged anything," Marcie demanded.

Emotionlessly, the Crenellian sat at the computer and started to work. "What have you done to my system?" he asked after a few heartbeats.

"We had to copy some information out of there. Just do what you need to do to pull up the system status."

"It'll take some time. I need to reboot." The alien went through the system, conducting both soft and hard boots of it. He went from station to station, before working his way back to where he started. Terry continued to pace. Dokken watched him as each time the colonel reached the large German Shepherd, he reached down and scratched Dokken's ears.

When the screen finally came up, Marcie breathed a sigh of relief. She half-expected the system to be dead after its conversation with Smedley. General Smedley Butler could be demanding at times, as well as not very gentle.

"The system has fired its plasma beam weapons, its projectile systems, the laser systems, but it has not fired any missiles. Wait a moment. It has taken significant damage. Ten percent of its armaments have been neutralized. Make that eleven percent."

"That's why Kae isn't answering. He's tearing that combat system a new asshole," Terry said proudly.

Marcie smiled. "Can you show what the combat unit looks like, please? Is it modular, a fleet of vehicles, mechs, or what?"

The alien tapped his screen and The Beast appeared. "It is a self-contained, single combat system, optimized for open terrain worlds like Tissikinnon Four. We had it on standby, just in case the Tiskers failed to keep their side of the bargain."

"Walk softly and drive a big tank," Terry whispered as he studied the weapon. "That looks like an Ogre."

"We call it Ground Assault System Four—Open Terrain."

"You call it GASFOT? That would be funny if we were in New York, but my son's out there fighting with that thing. There has to be a way to shut it down." Terry put his hand on the alien's small shoulders. The Crenellian looked at the hand, but didn't do anything about it.

"There is not. Our systems are built with a failsafe that the weapon will continue the assault without instruction, in case the operations center is destroyed or otherwise compromised."

"That's fucked up," Terry said, scowling darkly. "That's terrorist-level bullshit. Final solution, your knucklehead leader said? That's really fucked up. I think Char was right. You fuckers are the galaxy's douchebags. Every planet has them, and it was inevitable that the galaxy would have them, too. It sucks that it's you, and we're working for you, but that is an issue in my control that I aim to resolve forthwith."

1 8

Fleeter had to duck as well as bend her knees severely to fit in the passageway. She figured out quickly that these were maintenance shafts and that The Beast was never intended to carry personnel, even those as tiny as the Crenellians.

"Come on, you little bitch, tell me your secrets," she pleaded with the mechanical monster. She traversed the tank from one side to the other and then decided that she would head aft. In an unmanned system, she figured there would be as much armor as possible between a potential enemy and the brains of the weapon.

She expected to find a computer terminal. If it didn't look like what they had on the *War Axe*, then she didn't know what to look for. She hoped it was obvious. The more she crawled through The Beast, the more worried she became.

Two grenades and a knife, she thought. *How can this suck more?*

SLUGS PINGED from the tank's armor as the Podder army maintained a steady volume of fire despite their staggering losses.

The tank's energy beams were wiping out wide swaths of Podders. Kae and his team were attacking the weapons as they fired, creating some spectacular explosions. Not all of the weapons died easily.

The tank was an armored behemoth, and it wasn't going quietly. The Beast jerked and bucked in an attempt to throw its riders from its back.

The magnetic boot locks kept the mechs steady, but the wild gyrations slowed their movement to better firing positions. Kae was surprised that such an immense vehicle could move as it did.

And the Podders kept coming. Wave upon wave, throwing their bodies into the line of fire.

I really need you to shut this thing down, Kae told Fleeter.

Working on it, she replied.

Work faster.

The mechs' railguns barked and spit. Molten shrapnel flew in wide arcs from weapon mounts that refused to give way. Duncan's suit was the first to redline. He saw the warning almost too late. He took two steps and ducked. Then the suit powered down. He stayed inside the suit, praying that the sun would brighten.

Praeter was next and then Cantor. Each locked up and remained where they were. The tank couldn't fire at them, but they couldn't fire either.

Kaeden hadn't been engaged as they had, but his red

light was flashing. On the ground in the distance, he could see the power supply they had to dump when The Beast attacked them.

It wasn't a question of who, but when. They needed it now, so Kaeden ran for the edge of the tank and jumped off, staying low to the ground to avoid the largest of the energy weapons. He zigzagged anew, accelerating toward the power supply, swinging wide as he ran past and picked it up with one hand, but it threw his balance off.

Kae stumbled and stopped for only a moment to get his feet under him.

The kinetic round hit him in the chest, throwing him through the air as the power supply tumbled from his armored hand. The light on his HUD burned a solid red for a moment before the suit powered down. Kaeden gasped for air as he lay on his back, trapped within the suit.

KIMBER USED her small comm device to summon three of the drop ships. They had secreted themselves away from the action. Armored, but unarmed, they were strictly for transporting the company. If the *War Axe* had been able to remain in orbit, the drop ships could have ferried equipment and resupply back and forth from the planet's surface.

The shuttles were boxy, about fifteen meters long, five meters wide, with stubby, high-mounted wings. They were flown by an Entity Intelligence, but had a manual mode, too. They had a rear ramp instead of a door because of their cargo purpose in addition to ferrying personnel.

With a fourteen-hundred-kilometer jaunt, there was no reason to walk.

The small shuttles approached quickly, flying low to the ground, the EI controlling them using tactical procedures to minimize the effectiveness of ground fire. Even though the enemy wasn't active, the entire area had been declared a combat zone.

The drop ships slowed, flared, and two of them landed softly. The third turned and raced in the direction that Terry and Char had gone.

"Load up!" Kimber called. Timmons and his people held their ground within the cavern, firing randomly into the tunnels as the platoon scrambled up the wall and outside. "First and second squads!"

Kimber pointed to the first shuttle. The third squad leader waved his people to the second shuttle.

Kim cupped her hands around her mouth. "Timmons, Joseph, let's go!" she yelled into the hole in the ground. The canister had been emptied, packs were stuffed to overflowing, and the vehicle had been buttoned up, just in case they'd be able to recover it later.

Waste not, want not, but if they had to leave it behind, they'd bill the client for the cost. Kimber didn't worry about it in either case because they hadn't finished the war, yet.

Joseph, Petricia, and the Podder climbed up the steep slope. For having stumpy legs and a wide shell, the alien was surprisingly agile, looking to have no problem at all getting itself out of the hole.

Next up, Timmons, Sue, Shonna, and Merrit fired a final volley before racing toward the slope and out of the hole. Kimber pointed toward the second shuttle where the Podder was climbing aboard.

She frowned as she watched because the Podder made for a tight squeeze. Timmons and Sue ran up the shuttle's rear deck and jumped, landing on Bundin's shell. He reached out his tentacle arms so they could grab on.

Shonna and Merrit followed suit and the four rode on the Podder. The rear deck closed as Kimber continued to watch.

"Did we adopt that guy?" she asked. A slug hit her in the back. Shocked out of her reverie, she bolted for the first shuttle.

"GET ON!" Terry demanded. The Were had changed back into human form and had already boarded the drop ship. Terry could see the other two shuttles approaching. The fourth shuttle remained concealed in a valley far away and would pick up Kaeden and his people when they were ready.

The Crenellians had different ideas. They understood the concept of mobile combat, but never accepted the premise that it meant they had to move.

"Get the fuck in there!" Terry screamed at the bald alien. Tik'Po'Rout stood there without changing his facial expression. Eight other Crenellians were equally stoic. Terry loomed and waved a fist in the leader's face.

Char was losing patience. Christina's was already gone. She clenched and unclenched her fists, waiting for the word to beat one of the Crenellians senseless.

Marcie walked casually into the group of aliens and picked two up, one under each arm, and boarded the shuttle. Char grabbed two, Christina wrapped two up, and Terry swept up the last three.

He dumped his three in the shuttle and stood at the edge of the ramp after he ordered it to close, in case one of the Crenellians ran for it.

But they didn't. "What's with you guys? You act fearless but then when it comes to any kind of physical engagement, you're useless."

"We don't fight," the first alien replied.

"I gathered that. What's your name?"

"I am Ankh'Po'Turn," he replied.

"Well, Ankh, we're going to see your buddies and then we're going to have a conversation, and then we're going to destroy every Crenellian computer on this planet if your boys don't stop the war."

"My name is Ankh'Po'Turn. We told you that the failsafe is to keep fighting. If you destroy the computers, then the war machines will continue until there is no life left on this planet," the Crenellian said.

"Why would anyone build such a thing, Ankh? Back on Earth, we used to have a concept called mutually assured destruction, and you know what we found out? MAD was valid. When the nukes started flying, everyone lost. It was bad. Out here in the universe, a gazillion miles from home, we find the same stupid shit. SMEDLEY!"

"Yes, Colonel Walton," the EI answered through the ship's speakers.

"Any progress with the Crenellian database?"

"Yes." Smedley did not expound.

Terry rolled his eyes. "Maybe there's something you could share with me, make me feel like our efforts have had some value?"

"The schematics are incomplete, but we have enough to send to Team BMW for further analysis."

"That's not very motivating," Terry said, frowning. He held Char's hand as they flew, something he'd been doing for nearly as long as they'd been together. They held hands like teenagers, two parts of one whole.

"I guess we'll just have to get you more data," Char added. "I'm sure the headquarters will have details that the outpost was lacking."

Terry nodded. The Crenellians remained impassive, standing where they'd been deposited within the shuttle. They shifted as the ship flew close to the ground, maintaining an irregular flight profile to foil air defense systems.

"Marcie, get a hold of Kae and find out what's going on," Terry ordered.

TH closed his eyes and rested his head on Char's shoulder. She leaned into him and both soon fell asleep.

"YOU SUCK!" Fleeter screamed her frustration within the bowels of The Beast. She had been from front to back and side to side, crawling as fast as she could, and had not found a single thing that looked like it was important.

Large sections of the tank were solid and blocked her access. She assumed what she was looking for was somewhere in those sealed areas.

You don't need to get in there. You only need to get the grenade in there, she told herself as she skirted the section in the middle of the tank. It was where she would have put anything important.

The air was stale without ventilation. The greater she exerted herself, the more tiring it became. The noise of battle dulled. Ammunition racks cycled, power generators buzzed and crackled, the tank's drive motors whined as they pushed the massive vehicle across the Poddern landscape.

Fleeter sat in the small corridor and sighed heavily. *Only close my eyes for a moment,* she negotiated with herself, but the volume of fire continued. Her delay was costing lives.

If she didn't use the grenades, then she guaranteed the assault would continue. The Beast continued to sow wanton death.

She yelled her anger, trying to summon the adrenaline to give her energy. She looked high and low, finally finding a gap near the low ceiling. Fleeter tried to look into it, but couldn't tell how far it went. She had no better option.

She pulled the pin and thrust the grenade through. She heard it clank against something and rattle on its way downward. She scooted down the passageway, around the corner, and as far in the other direction as she could go.

The explosion came as a low rumble that soon died away.

"Fuck," she complained, sitting down.

And then the tank heaved as secondary explosions rattled the vehicle. Fleeter pulled the hood of her ship suit over her head as the fireball billowed around the corner, filling the corridor in both directions.

SOMEWHERE IN THE vast Federation

"Mister President," Nathan said with a big smile. "I'm so pleased that you took my call."

The Crenellian president looked at the screen, but didn't move. Nathan wondered if the image had frozen until someone walked past in the background.

"I'll get to the point because clearly, you are a busy man. It has been brought to my attention that there are planetary defensive systems getting used against the Bad Company and that they are of Crenellian manufacture. We will need the codes to disable them to continue our operations."

"No," the president replied. "We need you to destroy those systems utterly, so the Tiskers lose their access to them."

Nathan rubbed his jaw. "You sold weaponry to Tissikinnon Four, and now you need us to destroy that weaponry. That was not in the contract, Mister President. Our mission is to end the war, not conduct a hardware purge."

"Destroying that hardware will help you achieve your goal. Honestly, if I had known that I was hiring amateurs, then there would have been no contract at all," the president answered.

Nathan leaned closer to the monitor. "Mister President, once our people take care of business on Tissikinnon Four, they'll be coming to visit you, so you can personally explain your duplicity. I doubt they'll accept your flippant answers and your arrogance. If you want to be the galaxy's arms dealer, that's your business, but when we go up against your equipment, that becomes our business. What if we shared samples of all your hardware and the codes to crack them with everyone in the Federation? How well do you think your business would do then?"

"You wouldn't. You don't have the codes," the president responded, still looking down his nose at the monitor.

"Our people are very resourceful. When they leave the planet, I expect they'll be carrying a full ship of your hardware, including all your computers." Nathan leaned back, took a drink of water, and then crossed his arms.

"They can take whatever they want from the Tiskers."

"That's not how this is going to work. They'll take it from the Crenellians because only their computers will have all the codes. You can disable the systems, or we'll take everything you own."

"I won't pay!" the president replied in a slightly elevated tone.

"I think you will. Once we have the equipment and the codes, you'll pay anything we ask to keep that from becoming public knowledge."

"That's blackmail. You're not a military for hire; you're a pack of criminals!"

"You hold onto that thought and see how it serves you when we put your entire dealings on full display before the bulk of the Federation. No one will be looking at us. All eyes will be on you and your shady dealings." Nathan stopped for a moment before continuing. "You know what

I like about you, Mister President? Not a goddamn thing. Have a nice day."

Nathan signed off. He had expected intransigence from the Crenellian president and didn't let it upset him.

He knew that Terry would take things differently, and Nathan decided that if the *War Axe* wanted to pay a visit to the Crenellian home world, no one would stop them.

Kaeden? Why aren't you answering? Marcie became more worried and frustrated with each attempt to contact her husband.

Praeter, Duncan, Cantor, can any of you hear me? she asked, using her comm chip, targeting the members of Kaeden's team.

Cantor here, ma'am. Me, Duncan, and Praeter are out of power. Gomez and Kelly are still fighting the tank. Capples took a hit and is down. Fleeter is out of her suit and inside the tank. There was a series of explosions just a few seconds ago. I hope they do the trick. This tank is a mother. Kaeden left the tank to get the power source. He's out there and down. We've moved where I can't see him any longer. I'm sorry. We're safe on the tank, but off of it, we're subject to the full firepower at its command.

Marcie didn't answer. She jumped up and worked her way to where Terry and Char were sitting. She shook them vigorously before yelling in their faces. "We have to go back!"

"What?" Terry mumbled. He'd fallen sound asleep in mere seconds and was struggling to come back to life.

"Kae is down. The others are out of power. There are only two out of the eight left fighting. We can't leave them like that."

Terry leaned forward, putting his head between his knees. "FUCK!" he yelled at the floor of the ship. He stood up, took a step toward the ramp, and pounded on it with his bare fist.

"You know that we can't go back," he whispered.

"Why the fuck not?" Marcie demanded.

"A tank. With air defenses, with anti-personnel weapon systems. If six of the eight mechs were put out of action by that thing, what would we be able to do?"

Marcie gritted her teeth and glared at her father-in-law. "That's my husband and the father of my children."

"He's my son, and they are all our people," Terry replied, grabbing her shoulder to hold it and look into her eyes. Marcie tried to shrug off his hand, but he held on tightly. "Our best option is to get those fuckers in their headquarters to shut the damn thing down."

Terry let go, and Marcie worked her way back to her seat, her head hung low.

Kaeden? Son? Terry tried his comm chip. He figured they would soon be out of range.

"Smedley, pick up the pace. I want to be at that headquarter ten minutes ago," Terry demanded. Smedley didn't bother answering. A small piece of the EI flew the ship, communicating with Smedley on the *War Axe* as needed.

Despite the seeming dichotomy, Smedley had been following the conversation within the drop ship and understood exactly what Terry Henry Walton was asking.

FLEETER WAITED for the smoke to clear, but it didn't. The corridors were filled with a dense black that boiled from the hole in the tank's mid-section. She listened and the machinery running The Beast seemed to slow, fewer engines were running. One weapon system continued to rage.

One of the energy weapons was drawing everything that the tank had to offer. The Beast had never planned on living forever, only sowing as much death and destruction as its power and stores could provide.

It was hurt, but it wasn't finished.

Fleeter crawled toward the sound, going by feel as she worked her way through.

She stopped and waved at the air, willing the smoke to clear, but it refused to go away. Her suit provided fresh air and for that, she was thankful. But like the powered, armored suits, supply was limited.

She checked the status meter on her forearm. Over an hour of air left. Plenty of time to figure out where to put the last grenade, but the longer she delayed, the more Podders that would die.

Fleeter fumbled her way forward, found the hum of the engine behind a panel that she couldn't move. She put the grenade next to it and then stopped.

She retraced her steps to find the transverse corridor. It

was farther than she thought. She crawled back to the power generator and felt around for a place to put the grenade. There weren't any. It was a blank wall.

"Fuck it." She turned her back and prepared to run. She pulled the pin and placed the grenade behind her. Fleeter let go and was off like a shot, scrambling and racing down the corridor. She rammed into something on her left, but kept going. She felt like the corner was coming up.

As she reached it, the grenade exploded.

MARCIE SAT DOWN. She wanted to cry out of frustration, but that wasn't her. She was a warrior first. Her husband was a warrior as well, and he had done what he had to do.

Just like her. She leaned back and took deep breaths, all the while glaring at the Crenellians. "I'll rip your heads off, you little fucking douchebags," she mumbled under her breath.

Christina put her hand gently on Marcie's leg. "We'll get them to shut it down. If not, then we'll do what we have to to kill every piece of equipment the dickheads have put on this planet."

Marcie stared at the Crenellian leader, who stared back. Her blood started to boil. Before Christina could stop her, Marcie lashed out with a fist, exploding the alien's nose across his face. He flew backwards. His people made no effort to catch him. He bounced off Aaron and Yanmei in the jump seats on the other side of the shuttle. They caught him and let him down gently, rolling him to his side so the unconscious leader wouldn't drown in his own blood.

Marcie sat back down.

"Feel better?" Christina asked.

Marcie smiled and shook her head. "Not really."

Christina put her lips close to Marcie's ear. "He deserved it," she whispered.

———

KAEDEN GROANED as he came to. The first thing he saw was a black cloud of smoke trailing into the sky from over the horizon. He tried to sit up, but his suit was powered down. He tried to boot it, but it still didn't have enough juice. If he leaned his head forward, he could see the power supply just out of arm's reach.

"Might as well be on another planet," he mumbled.

Cap, you there? Kaeden asked.

Thank the stars. We thought we'd lost you. Your suit showed that you were done, Capples replied.

Out here, lying on my back, like a turtle that's been flipped over. I could use a hand if someone's free.

We can't reach Fleeter, but there were some god-awful explosions from inside the tank. Kelly and Gomez are cleaning up the independent weapons systems right now. Once they have those killed, we'll be out to get you.

Thanks, Cap. Send Kelly to check on Fleeter. Let me try to contact the colonel.

Kae tried but couldn't reach any other member of the company using his comm chip. He expected that they had moved out of range, but hadn't known they were moving.

Cap, can you use your suit to contact the drop ships, see if our people are on board? Kaeden asked.

Will do. Standby.

Kae waited, checking what he could without power, which was limited to what he could physically see and what he could touch with a limited range of motion. When the suit was powered up, it filled airbags that pressed in around the form of the wearer. If the suit lost power, the bags deflated. Kae had inches of room to move, but not enough to do anything else. The back of the suit was on the ground. It was open, but Kae couldn't move the suit enough to get out.

"Personal log, Stardate twenty-four eleven point two. Invent a way to get out of a dead suit when you're on your back. In other news, the twilight sky over Tissikinnon Four is a beautiful auburn. Kaeden Walton, signing off," Kae said to himself. If he only had more time to watch television, because the *War Axe* archives had mesmerizing shows to watch. There wasn't enough time remaining in his long life to watch everything he wanted to watch.

If only he could get Marcie interested in *Star Trek* or *Battlestar Galactica*.

FLEETER TRIED TO CRAWL, but the pain in her leg was too great. She reached down to feel what the damage was, but found a puddle of blood where her lower leg used to be. Torn off at the knee, she used the shreds of her ship suit's lower leg to tie as a tourniquet.

She was getting lightheaded, but couldn't pass out. Her hood had been torn. Her suit was ripped and torn, a victim of the grenade's shrapnel. She coughed from the black smoke that continued to billow down the corridor.

Where's the way out? she asked. Fleeter used her arms to pull herself along, staying low to the floor where the clouds were less dense.

Fleeter rested every few feet, but not for long. Her lungs burned from the acrid air. Her nanocytes were taxed to the extreme trying to repair the damage to her leg while also keeping up with the damage being done to her lungs and eyes.

She found the ladder and gripped the bottom rung to lift herself into a sitting position. Then she grabbed the next rung and pulled. Her head swam and a wave of nausea overwhelmed her. She turned her head in time to puke most ingloriously back into the inside of the tank. She gagged, but reached for the next rung. She tugged with both hands pulling herself tightly to the ladder.

Wedged into the opening, she blocked the black smoke enough that fresh air blew over her. She breathed deeply as daggers of pain shot through her body. Something blocked the sun.

Or not. She blacked out and started to fall.

THE *WAR AXE*

"Get those suits on and get out there!" Commander Lagunov shouted with a big smile. His two volunteers waved as they hurried into the powered, armored suits.

All the bots were engaged and Blagun was adding the extra manpower to push the repair work over the hump.

He could feel in his bones that the hangar bay doors were almost fixed.

Not one, but *both* of them.

The captain appeared out of nowhere as the two hull techs clumped away in their suits, heading for the airlock to the side of the hangar bay doors. They squeezed in together and the hatch closed behind them. It cycled from green to red. Gravity disappeared from inside and the two floated into space before activating their pneumatic thrusters, sending them beyond the window.

"Keep us informed of their progress, Smedley," Micky requested.

The captain and the commander watched a view screen next to the airlock. Smedley brought the image up showing the outside of the ship, where the two technicians and six repair bots worked diligently on a warped area of metal at the joint where the door retracted into the hull.

Two of the bots were using plasma torches to cut a huge section away. The molten metal dripped and floated, cooling quickly, changing from orange to black and disappearing in the darkness of space.

The bots were plastered to the front of the ship as the *War Axe* continued to travel toward the fifth planet in the system. Micky had stopped the acceleration, but the ship was still moving rapidly through the vacuum of space.

The piece came free and the six bots moved in to pull it aside. The two technicians used the power of their mechs to adjust the piece. The bots with the plasma torches went back to work, trimming the cutout as one of the people in the suits indicated.

The bots trimmed, touched up, and trimmed some more.

"They cut it twice and it was still too short," Blagun joked.

Micky raised one eyebrow as he continued to watch the work outside. One of the bots secured the extra pieces. It wouldn't do to have them bounce down the ship until they hit the raised bridge section.

The suited figures wrestled the modified piece into place and four bots started welding.

"Keep me informed," Micky said as he started to walk away.

"That should do it, Captain. I was worried that piece wouldn't come free. I think we're in the clear and two days ahead of schedule. Damn! I see some of Jenelope's cake in my future."

Micky nodded with a tight smile. He wasn't sure if Blagun was using a euphemism or not.

Marcie grinned broadly, relieved at Capples's report. Terry got up and high-fived everyone in the shuttle, everyone except the Crenellians.

Terry stopped to check on their leader, who was still passed out. A small puddle of blood was starting to coagulate under Tik'Po'Rout's face.

"I'm not cleaning that up," Terry said, looking directly at Marcie. She shrugged one shoulder and grinned sheepishly. Christina covered her mouth, unsure if it was okay to laugh or not.

Cory finally took a knee next to the Crenellian. She held her hands over his face. The familiar blue glow appeared as her nanocytes transferred to the alien to fix the surface injuries where they could still draw power from their host.

The nose straightened and the bleeding stopped. When Cory looked up, Terry nodded and thanked her. "You were going to let him lie here, weren't you?"

"Yes," he answered. Cory furled her brows. "I'd have more choice words, but I refrain from using such language in polite company."

That earned Terry a bemused look from Char. "No shit?" she asked.

"I'm turning over a new leaf, beloved," Terry said, bowing. He turned to Marcie. "I couldn't be happier to hear that your husband is okay."

"Me, too," Marcie replied.

Terry worked his way to the front of the drop ship and accessed the main screen, a system that he'd had put into the shuttles so that he could brief the teams on their way into the landing zone. He pulled up a map of the site. It showed a nondescript area with no terrain features.

"Smedley? Can you show us any defensive systems in place around the Crenellian headquarters?"

"I will access that part of the data you provided," the EI replied. Terry looked to the Crenellians. Their eyes were fixated on the screens. "How much of your lives do you spend in front of a computer?"

Ankh'Po'Turn answered. "All of it."

"The luxury bathrooms and the fine dining kitchen? Those are to entice you to bathe and eat, otherwise, you'd remain within your computers, oblivious to the outside world."

The alien didn't answer. "You little fuckers can't relate to real people doing real things, can you?" Terry blurted.

"Turning over a new leaf, huh?" Char said.

"I'm a work in progress," Terry replied, smiling. "Thanks for that, Ankh. I'm starting to understand. We need to finish this so you can get back to your systems and do what you do. That's my promise to you."

Tik'Po'Rout played with his nose, confused that it was healed. "What's the matter, Tik? Not used to getting punched in the face?"

"My name is Tik'Po'Rout and no. I've never seen my own blood before."

"I wish I could say that," Terry mumbled. Char snickered, absentmindedly rubbing her head where she'd been shot earlier that day. Dried blood caked her hair. Terry's pants leg was shredded, but the bloodstains didn't show on the black of the uniform. He looked at the shuttle's occupants. They had all been injured and bled at some point on this operation while on Poddern.

"Now you have, my friend," Cory interjected. "But let's try not to get hurt again."

"I like her," the alien said. "You should try to be more like her."

Terry rolled his eyes and turned away, proud of his daughter and how she treated everyone with equal respect. He felt guilty for his "little fuckers" comment, but felt that he was right with the sentiment, but missed with the presentation of his discovery.

Smedley brought up the requested information.

"Son of a bitch," Terry lamented, looking at the overlays that appeared on the map. "Slow us down, Smedley. We don't want to fly into the middle of that."

Terry manipulated the screen using hand gestures to rotate, zoom in, and zoom out. A three-dimensional air defense zone with overlapping fields of fire were displayed. On the ground, the defenses showed interlocking fields of fire from hardened defensive positions using both plasma and kinetic weapons.

"Ankh, why would you set up such an extensive above-ground system when the Podders live underground?"

"We discovered that after the fact," the alien replied.

"Does that mean this system isn't in place?" Terry wondered.

"The computer thinks the system is in place."

Terry scratched his chin and pursed his lips as he calculated the risks of various assault scenarios. He refused to assume that the defensive system was not in place, which meant they needed to land more than twenty kilometers away and hike in.

More delays.

"Does your system discriminate between living species?" Terry asked.

CAPPLES CAUGHT Fleeter by the shoulder in his armored hand as her eyes rolled back in her head and she started to fall. He carefully pulled her out of the tube and placed her on the hull of the tank.

Gomez and Kelly cheered as the final weapon system exploded. Their armored boots clumped as they jumped up and down.

"Hey, you two, mind running out and picking up the major?" Capples asked. "And bring that power supply back here while you're at it!"

We'll have you up and running in no time, Cap told Praeter, Duncan, and Cantor using his comm chip.

With darkness descending, their only choice was to use the power supply to recharge sufficiently to make it through the night.

Gomez and Kelly ran across the tank and launched themselves into the air, landing with a resounding thump before running into the distance.

In less than three minutes, the power supply was running and Kaeden was upright and plugged in. Gomez picked up Kae and Kelly hoisted the power supply so they could return to the tank.

Cantor climbed out of his suit and ran to where Capples was crouching over Fleeter. Cantor was shocked to see that she was missing half a leg. He dove in and started adjusting the shredded suit leg to improve its use as a tourniquet.

"Holy shit," he said softly as blood covered his hands. He tightened the tie-off until the flow stopped.

A slug pinged off Capples's suit. He stood up to see where it came from. Another slug and then an entire volley hit him. He jumped past Cantor, but the Podder slugs tore through the unprotected man, the ship's suit not designed to stop bullets. As Cantor fell over from the damage, he angled himself to land on top of Fleeter, protecting her unconscious form with his riddled body.

A slug hit Cantor in the head, ending his life.

THE *WAR AXE*

The forcefield shimmered in place as the hangar bay doors retracted. Blagun cheered from within his ship suit as the immensity of space opened before him. Two technicians pulled themselves hand over hand down the access until they were even with the deck. They stepped down and then waved at the commander.

He gave them the double thumbs up. They disappeared back outside as they headed for the airlock to get back inside the ship. The repair bots moved to the next in a never-ending string of tasks on the outer hull.

"Well done," came Micky's voice over the ship-wide broadcast.

"We can recover the drop ships at any time, Captain," Commander Lagunov said, before walking toward the airlock to welcome his technicians back inside and congratulate them on a job well done.

The ship was still heading away from the planet, but Blagun liked to check things off his to-do list, and the doors were the biggest one and hanging over his head like a guillotine.

PODDERN

The three shuttles settled into place behind a small hill. The platoon and tactical teams disembarked. Even the Crenellians got off without having to be carried.

Terry walked up the hill, far enough to peer over the top. He couldn't see the headquarters or anything that wasn't a natural part of the landscape.

Tik and Ankh joined Terry on the hillside because Cory was holding their hands and leading them.

"How far away is it?" Tik asked.

"Twenty kilometers," Terry replied. "You don't know how far that is, do you?"

"Of course, I know how far that is in our measuring system," the alien leader said, standing up straight and looking down his nose.

"Not out here you don't. How far away is that hill to our left?" Terry asked.

Tik looked at it, looked up at Terry Henry, and then looked down at the ground.

"As I suspected. Stay behind us and keep up," Terry ordered and headed down the hill to meet the others.

Kimber had the platoon formed in a defensive perimeter, but Terry waved at her to bring them all in.

vampires, a Podder, werewolves, weretigers, Crenellians, and a myriad of nano-enhanced humans.

"Listen up, people. It'd be nice if we could blast the place from orbit, but we can't do that because the failsafe is utter annihilation of the Podders. We need to capture this headquarters and convince the Crenellians within to shut down their weapon systems or at least give us access so Smedley can dig into the ones and zeroes."

Terry looked at the determined faces, wondering how many would make it. "You saw the defensive systems that surround this place. It looks intimidating, but don't be afraid. We work from a position of power. Anything fires from inside there, mass the railgun firepower against it. Take it out and move on. Keep your helmets on your heads and present the lowest profile target you can. Make yourselves small and deadly."

Terry drew in the dirt to create a map of what they were up against.

"Timmons, werewolf it in from the right flank. Marcie, go with Aaron, take your people and weretiger your way from the left flank. Joseph, vamp it up behind us and try to keep Bundin from getting wiped off the planet. We will need you to tap the minds of the Crenellians in case they don't see things our way, so don't get yourself killed on the way.

"We don't have much time. I expect the tank that Kaeden attacked isn't the only one out there. There's probably a fleet of behemoths destroying entire Pods. I won't allow a genocide, not as long as I'm still breathing. I can't ever hate anyone that much, except maybe some Forsaken, but even that hatred burned me up inside..."

"Then we need to win this one," Marcie said. "And fast, too. Kimber, carry those guys. We run in two minutes, V formation, two up, one back, all out. It'd be nice to get there before it's completely dark out here."

"Let's not burn any more of our precious daylight. OORAH!" Kim shouted. The platoon replied in kind with a hearty round of battle cries. Joseph talked constantly with Bundin, but gave the thumbs up that they were ready. Petricia nodded slightly, hesitating as she hadn't bought into the plan.

Timmons, Sue, Shonna, and Merrit stripped, bundled their clothes and threw them inside the shuttle before changing into werewolf form. The weretigers and Christina followed suit. She chose her Pricolici form, since it was deadlier than the werewolf. That form allowed her to carry the railguns to add firepower to the attack.

Terry, Char, and Dokken took the point and started jogging toward their objective. The Were and their teams flared out to the flanks, building speed and increasing the distance between the three groups. The platoon members carried the nine Crenellians, who seemed to enjoy the ride, although they didn't show it on their faces.

"There might be some hope for the Crooners yet."

"Crooners?" Char said as they slowly accelerated.

"You know I can't do three-syllable names and four is out of the question. So, Tik, Ankh, and Crooners."

"So let it be written," Char intoned. "So let it be done."

"GET UP THERE!" Kaeden yelled. "Put me down and get in the fight."

Kae's suit had enough juice that he powered up, so he could carry the power supply as it charged. The cloud of slugs that passed over the tank suggested that the Podders were fighting back against the dead tank, mistaking the mechs for Crenellians.

Or not and they were attacking anyone not from Poddern.

"We saved your dumb asses!" Kaeden bellowed using the suit's external speakers. He found his way to the tank, but the Podders were streaming around the sides, firing their slug-throwers. The slugs were pinging from the power supply and Kae couldn't risk that getting damaged. He shoved it between two road wheels of the massive tank's tracks and leveled his railgun, but hesitated to pull the trigger.

The volume of fire increased. His suit withstood it all. He turned off his microphones from outside the suit.

"I gave you a chance," he whispered and started to fire,

aiming center mass on the Podders' shell in an attempt to take them out with one shot.

There were too many of them, and Kae opened up in rapid-fire mode. If he had his microphones turned on, he would have discovered the rest of his team was doing the same thing.

TERRY PLAYED with his JDS as he ran, dialing it back and forth between three and eleven.

"Be careful with that thing. You'll put an eye out," Char said, laughing.

They ran at a pace that would quickly eat up the distance.

"I can't just dial it to eleven and destroy the entire head-quarters. That would be the easy answer, but the Crooners aren't going to make it easy on us. I detest their thinking, although I'm doing it, too. Destroy them all and be done with it!"

"They are detached from reality. They don't look their enemies in the face. From a computer's standpoint, isn't the best option to eliminate an enemy? They've removed the humanity from the process, which means that their sense of justice is distorted," Char explained.

"That's what I was thinking. They simply don't know, and it's up to us to educate them. I wonder what this bunch will have to say to their fellows."

"Does our whole plan rest on our boys here playing nice?" Char asked.

"I have co-equal plans in mind. I want to get Smedley

into their system. I also want this bunch to inform the headquarters people about the errors of their ways."

"I'm counting on Smedley," Char replied.

"As am I, lover."

Terry and Char had a millisecond to react as the plasma beam lashed toward them. Their random direction changes on their approach saved their lives. They both sped up, zigzagging as they accelerated as if the fires of damnation were licking at their feet.

The plasma beams were probably hotter.

The platoon broke apart, aimed their railguns, and fired at the weapon platforms that materialized from beneath the dirt. As Terry spotted the towers popping up, he dialed the JDS to ten and let loose. With each shot, a tower was vaporized. He stopped running, took a knee, and braced himself to fire.

Finally, the Podders stopped coming. Kae picked up the power supply and climbed atop the tank. He set it next to Praeter and plugged him in. Kaeden shined his suit lights around the area. None of the Podders had made it onto the tank. They'd remained on the ground as they fired at those on The Beast.

Kaeden took a deep breath and surveyed the damage. Fleeter was down,lying in a pool of blood. Cantor lay dead on top of her. Kae carefully moved the man to the side. Fleeter was ashen and breathing shallowly. He looked at the field tourniquet but didn't touch it. He didn't want the stump of her leg to start bleeding again.

"Report," Kaeden said wearily.

Gomez replied first. "I need to recharge. I'm flashing red."

"Me, too," Kelly added. "I don't know how many Podders are down, but it's a lot."

Kae heard the clump of armored boots as someone

walked across the top of the tank. "Duncan is okay, just needs to be charged up. He's been trapped in there for, well damn, I don't know how long," Gomez said.

Capples walked up next to Kaeden. He powered down and climbed out of his suit. He ran a hand through his tangle of hair as he looked at Cantor's body.

"Invincible, just until we're not," he whispered.

"Are we clear? There is no threat?" Kae asked.

"They're gone, but they didn't retreat. I think they're all dead. My suit light shows a blue sea with nothing moving. I don't know where they came from, and if any retreated, I don't know where to," Kelly said, sounding exhausted.

"Bring it in. Fleeter could use some company," Kaeden ordered. "You can get out of your suits, but stay low. I'll stay armored up."

The mechs moved close, faced outboard, and powered down. The individuals climbed out, shoulders hunched and heads sagging. Even with the suit augmentations, the warrior within still had to move and engage.

Kae kept his suit light on, having it act almost like a campfire, but there was no singing. There was no joy.

"The Bad Company mech platoon acquitted itself well, but there will be no battle streamer from this fight. We left one of our own on this battlefield. We'll carry another off. We ran out of power before the battle was joined. What a debacle."

"That didn't get Cantor killed. The fucking Podders attacked us as if we were the bad guys! We just killed their enemy, but still they came. Fuck those blue stalk-heads."

"I have to agree. We'd been running all out for two

days? Three days? I don't even know anymore. You ran out of power twice," Kelly said, pointing to Kaeden.

"If there ever was an untenable position, ours was it, yet we still managed to pull through. Fleeter is a fucking hero. She climbed in the guts of that thing and killed it," Capples added. "And Cantor, too. His suit died, but he didn't stop fighting. He climbed out to help her and you saw it when you came up here. He used his body to shield her. That's what a real fucking warrior does. Honor. Courage. Commitment. He lived that and so did she."

"We all do," Praeter suggested. "We didn't back away from the fight, sir. We took it to 'em."

Kaeden nodded, and a tear trailed down one cheek. "Cantor is the first of the mechs to die, and he won't be the last, but let it be said, he died with honor, in the service of his fellow mech warriors. I say it's time to call in the drop ship, get the medical supplies we need for Fleeter. Then we'll bed down there for the night and go find the others first thing in the morning."

"Aye, aye, sir," Capples replied.

Kae's suit comm crackled to life. "Kae, we're kind of pinned down and could use a little of your horsepower. Are you able to join us?" Char asked her son.

"On our way, Mom. I'm sure our ship has the coordinates."

"Smedley will bring you right to us," Char said. Kae could hear railguns barking in the background. "You may have to do an air drop as the Crenellians have a robust three-dimensional engagement zone over top of their headquarters. We can't destroy the building or the computers, only the weapon systems."

"Understand. We lost Cantor and Fleeter lost her leg. I'm down two, but the rest of us will be there. Look for the flares and you'll know we're on our way down," Kae reported before signing off and summoning the drop ship.

"Time to go, people. Load up as much power as you can get because we're going back into combat, only as soon as humanly possible."

DOKKEN CROUCHED to the ground as Terry and Char stayed low on either side of him. After Terry's decimation of the towers, the low-profile guns came out. They fired parallel to the ground using a rapid fire, like a machine gun. In the darkness, the muzzle flashes and zings, and the bullets whipping past, put everyone on the ground. Timmons had stalled on the right flank for the same reason, while Marcie's group on the left flank were trying to take advantage of a shallow runoff channel to crawl into the compound and attack the guns from behind.

In the interim, everyone was dug in, trying to worm their way into the best covered positions. The Crenellians watched with great interest, while the Podder found a shaft and disappeared underground.

Bundin asked Joseph to tell the others not to follow him because the tunnels could be dangerous. This wasn't his Pod and he couldn't be certain of the stability or hospitality.

Joseph and Petricia waited by the hole.

Char reached into the Etheric dimension to see what there was to see, if anything was hiding underground, but she found only one Podder moving slowly and assumed it was Bundin.

Terry couldn't lay still. He twitched and moved. "Get some rest," Char said, realizing that it was a useless thing to say as soon as the words left her mouth.

"I hate this," Terry said as he carefully aimed his Jean Dukes Special, waited for a muzzle flash, and fired. He gave his best evil laugh when the weapon station exploded with spectacular fireworks.

But two more weapons opened up and honed in on Terry's position. He draped an arm over Dokken as he tried to become one with the dirt, while Char did the same thing on the other side.

"I really hate this," Terry reiterated.

MARCIE CRAWLED FORWARD at an agonizingly slow pace. She had her arms far in front of her, pulling herself along while pushing with her toes. She scraped along, digging a small ditch where her equipment was dragging. Her pack was in a hole at the rally point that she'd designated well to their rear. Her railgun was over her arm as she had the sling wrapped between her thumb and forefinger.

She maintained a profile that didn't stick up more than eight inches from the ground, about the depth of the channel she crawled through. Behind her, the weretigers crouched and stayed still. The four warriors were dug in around them. If Marcie had been able to run, she would have covered the ground in seconds, but crawling was a miserably slow way to travel.

But the withering fire that the Crenellians had set up would have put a damper on any direct assault.

It already did, but it would have ruined a lot of people's days had Terry tried to press the attack instead of going to ground and waiting for the mechs to show up.

"Can I use your comm?" Terry asked. Char handed over her device to link her to the drop ship.

"What happened to yours?" Char asked. Terry pointed to the pocket on his flak jacket where the slugs had torn it apart. "You kept it out in the open?"

"Why are you surprised? It's the same place I've kept it for, well damn, two hundred years, I guess."

"About how long it's been since you last took a shower. You stink," Char added lovingly.

"I'd bag on you for werewolf smell, but then my chances of getting a two-person shower when we get back to the ship will probably be vastly reduced," Terry replied.

Char nodded, while surreptitiously smelling inside her shirt and finding that it wasn't all Terry.

I could have told you that, Dokken interjected.

"Don't you start!" Char cautioned, ducking her head as a new wave of incoming fire swept over their position.

"Kaeden, are you airborne yet?" Terry asked into the small comm device.

"We just loaded up. We have four suits that needed to be carried, and two people," Kaeden said sadly.

"We've seen people die before, but we can't lament their loss until after the battle has been won," Terry suggested.

"It's not just our people, Dad. We wiped out an entire army of Podders. They didn't stand a chance."

"Did they give you any option?"

"Not really. After we killed the tank, they kept coming and we were running out of power. I don't know what they could do to a person inside a dead suit." Kae replied.

"Justice is not an easy export, and those on the receiving end may deserve it more than others. Or they may deserve it less. It is incumbent upon us to protect those who shouldn't be on the receiving end at all.

"If I understand the Pod boundaries, the one you destroyed is the same one that wiped out the Crooners who were mining according to the contract they had with those very same Podders. When they did that, they headed down a path of self-destruction. It is my opinion that this Pod committed suicide, using the Crooners and you as their weapons. Does it make any sense to keep attacking an enemy down to your very last man, using the same tactics and ineffective weapons?"

Kaeden didn't answer right away. Terry started to wonder if they'd been cut off.

"On our way. ETA is fifteen minutes. The drop ship is accelerating toward the upper atmosphere. We'll be there soon, Dad. Whaddya say we end this thing and go home? I'm looking forward to some private time with my wife."

Terry looked toward Char. She peeked one sparkling purple eye over the top of Dokken's long hair. "I hear that. See you soon."

All hands, all hands. Colonel Terry Henry Walton coming to you live with a mouth full of dirt. The mech platoon is on their way in. They are going to jump into the middle of the enemy compound and take out those weapons. Do not expose yourself before then. When the all-clear is sounded, run like hell and rally at the headquarters entrance. I suspect it's buried in the middle there somewhere, but we'll find it, and then we'll go have us a little conversation. Team leaders, report, Terry said using his comm chip.

The team leaders reported in, one by one starting with Timmons, then Kimber, Joseph, Aaron, and Marcie. Ramses piped up too, although he wasn't a team lead at present. He was in charge of making sure the small support crew of Cory and Auburn were safe.

Ten minutes to touch down, people. Stay frosty.

"You love saying that," Char added.

"It's one of the best Space Marine lines ever!"

"Said by actors who weren't Marines," Char countered.

"Said by a Marine in combat with actual aliens," Terry added definitively, pressing his face into the dirt as an energy beam raged overhead. "Where did that thing come from? I thought we killed all of those."

Terry waited and then looked over the small berm he'd pushed in front of his position. From the muzzle flashes, he could make out a new tower, or newly repaired old tower. He couldn't be sure.

"I'll be damned. The little fuckers have some resilience. Check that. Their equipment has some resilience. I can't wait to hear how Kae and his people took out that behemoth of a tank." Terry slid his pistol to the front, checked the setting, aimed, and turned the JDS loose.

He chuckled as the tower erupted in a gout of flame.

22

Bundin found a way in. We can join him through the tunnels, Joseph said.

Terry tried to look behind him, but the darkness was absolute. He couldn't see where he needed to run, and there was too much open space. The mech unit would be arriving soon, and Terry expected all hell to break loose.

You and Petricia go, take any you need from the platoon who are close enough to you to minimize their exposure to fire in addition to your own warriors, Terry replied.

Just taking Petricia and my four. Everyone else is too far away.

Godspeed, Joseph, and be ready. Shit is going to start blowing up with great frequency very soon.

"Bundin found a way in, so Joseph is taking his team underground," Terry told Char. She nodded slightly.

I have to pee, Dokken said.

"Unless you want to lay in it, I suggest you wait five minutes," Terry replied.

Is that what you did?

"No. I dug a hole," Terry replied.

"I held it because I'm an adult," Char added.

From high above in the middle of the darkened sky, rockets streamed downward. Terry watched their trails as they spiraled toward the ground. Rapid projectile fire raced upward to meet them. Two exploded midair, but the others made it through.

Terry ducked his head, as did Char and Dokken. The rockets hit in a pattern that blanketed the compound. A huge fireball from the combined explosions billowed skyward. Terry looked up in time to see six shadows drop through the fireballs, using their pneumatic jets to slow themselves as they approached the ground.

Their impact shook the ground. Moments later, the railguns opened up.

KAEDEN and the others fired their railguns on the way down to help slow themselves.

It didn't really work. Kae grunted when he hit the ground, an instant feeling of being hit by a train. The suit compensated and he returned to himself quickly, as did the others. They fired at the weapon emplacements from behind.

What is it with these guys that they don't have any internal security? Kae thought. Just like on the tank, none of the weapons faced inboard. *The final solution protocol. If the computers are destroyed, they need to have a safe place while their weapons scorch the remaining life from the planet.*

Kae appreciated the vulnerability, while hating the reason it was created.

"Flashing red," Kelly reported.

"Same here," Praeter said. One by one, they reported their limitations. Kaeden was close, but still energized.

The power supply remained on the drop ship hovering at a safe altitude directly over the compound.

"Finish it!" Kae called and started to jog in a circle around the compound, killing the automated weapons as he passed, while the others saw their systems drop in power until they shut everything off to save enough in case of an emergency. They had learned that running to redline could have dangerous consequences.

When Kae was finished, the Crenellian emplacements were interlocking smoking ruins. Kae stood tall, holding his railgun over his head as he cheered, to himself.

One step closer to finishing it all, if the colonel was right about this headquarters being the lynchpin of the operation.

THE BATTLE WAS brief before both silence and darkness returned. "ALL CLEAR!" Kaeden shared using his suit's speakers cranked to maximum. Shortly after that, Queen belted out *We Are the Champions*.

"Is this where we run like hell?" Char asked as she stood and dusted herself off. She smiled at her husband, before making like she was going to sprint ahead.

"No plan survives first contact," Terry replied, brushing himself off. "I think we shall take a more dignified approach." He strolled ahead two steps to avoid Dokken relieving himself. Terry looked back, took one more step, and then started to run.

Char bolted after him. Dokken trotted, with his head held high. Getting there first wasn't one of his priorities. He wanted the humans to finish this because his thoughts kept drifting back to the *War Axe*, where his arch enemy had free run of the ship.

MARCIE WAS happy and pissed at the same time. All of the worm-crawling she did to cover a grand total of fifty yards. Her hair was soaked with sweat and matted to her head because of the helmet.

The weretigers bounded past her along with the Pricolici and the four warriors as they ran toward the area illuminated by the armored suit lights.

She wiped her head on her sleeve and ran after them, hurrying to catch up. They were the first ones to arrive after the mechs had cleared everything out.

The weretigers sniffed at the destroyed equipment and circled as if confused. Christina turned her head back and forth as if almost hearing something but not quite.

Marcie found Kaeden as he finished ordering the drop ship to land at the edge of the compound. He looked down at his wife and held out an armored hand. She took it, but wanted him out of the suit.

"No can do," he whispered to her. "I'm the only one with any power. We need to fix that issue, by the way, when we do our hot wash."

A *hot wash*, the after-action review that they'd conduct as soon as possible after the operation finished.

"Maybe we can get Ted to work on it," Marcie offered, disappointed that Kae would stay suited up.

The drop ship settled into position. *Cory, see what you can do for Fleeter? She's hurt badly,* Kae told his sister using the comm chip.

The werewolves were next to arrive, then Terry and Char with the platoon. Dokken trotted up ahead of Ramses, Cory, and Auburn, who turned to intercept the drop ship as the ramp started to lower. Cory rushed inside.

Terry and Char walked around the compound, looking at the destroyed weaponry. "The limitation of stationary defenses," Terry said. "Someone is always going to have better firepower, or they'll just bypass your stuff."

"The Crenellians are advanced when it comes to the technology of warfare, but not when it comes to the tactics," Kaeden offered from his armored suit, seeing the platoon arrive carrying nine of the aliens. They were put down where they stood, mildly interested in the destruction around them.

Praeter and Duncan slowly pounded past as they headed for the drop ship in order to access the power supply. Gomez and Kelly were close behind. Capples stayed in low power mode, waiting his turn.

Char used her senses to find the door. Kaeden made quick work of removing the dirt from around it. Dokken sniffed at it as the Were pack circled. Christina was near the front. Terry signaled for her to follow him. Kae grabbed the handle with one hand and counted down with the other.. When he reached zero, he yanked.

And didn't move. He braced himself and pulled again.

"This one's a little more robust than the outpost door, it appears," Marcie said.

"Thermite!" Terry called and held his hand out.

No one slapped a thermite grenade into it. He turned in a slow circle. "AUBURN!" Terry yelled.

Auburn emerged from the shuttle and jogged to where Terry was standing. "I need a thermite grenade."

"We didn't bring any," Auburn replied, holding his hands up to calm TH. "When we did the initial planning to come down here, we were supposed to be fighting the populace of Tissikinnon Four, which is a barely industrialized society. We never intended on fighting the advanced systems that the Crenellians have because they never told us that's what we were up against."

Terry pursed his lips and whistled. "Fair enough," Terry replied before turning to face the others. "Options!"

"Rocket," Kae said. "I have one left and it's not doing any good hanging off my back."

"Grenades," someone called out.

"Those will just bounce off," Kae answered.

"Explosives," another shouted. "Sorry, these are for excavation work."

"Sounds like your rocket, Kae. I'll hold the JDS as a last resort because we want to minimize damage inside the complex," Terry said, stroking his chin in thought. "Clear the area to one hundred meters."

People and Were alike scrambled for cover. The platoon picked up the Crenellians and carried them to safety.

Terry and Char headed for the drop ship. Marcie was already there, holding Fleeter's hand.

Cory was covered with a blanket as she slept in the jump seats. Char touched her daughter's head, lovingly smoothing her hair over her wolf ear. Besides the silver streak of hair that framed one side of her face, Cory's gift from her mother had been wolf ears. Cory was not a werewolf, which made her ears even more of an anomaly.

Terry watched his wife and daughter, while also finding himself looking longingly at the jump seat bed. He had slept there a number of times and found it as comfortable as a hammock. He couldn't blame her for sleeping, not after she expended her energy healing the injured warrior.

The leg was growing back, being reassembled at the nano level.

Fleeter was asleep too, as her body shepherded all of its energy toward the damage.

"She'll be fine," Ramses said from the other side of a dead mech suit.

"That's good news, thank you," Terry said, feeling tired as the body bag with Cantor's remains propped in a corner weighed on him. Terry stared at it before shaking himself free.

He looked longingly at the mech suits, but with four people trying to recharge at once, there was no time to bring those two systems up to speed.

He wasn't going to get his shot driving the mech. Not that day and not for a while.

"FIRE IN THE HOLE!" Kae called the standard Force de Guerre warning from near the drop ship. The rocket whooshed away. There was a ten-second delay as the weapon raced upward before turning and attacking its target from directly above. The rocket hit with a fantastic scream, exploding to send a shockwave in all directions. The ship bucked once before settling back down.

Kae ran to the hatch. "It's not looking good," he said. Terry sighed as he took Char's hand and together, they walked off the ship.

JOSEPH SHINED A FLASHLIGHT. The tunnel was as dark as a Stygian night. Even his Vampiric senses could discern nothing in the blackness. He could feel Bundin close by.

I see a doorway, Bundin said, maintaining a monologue for Joseph's benefit. Joseph couldn't talk back unless he was in physical contact, but the Podder knew that the group followed because of his exceptional hearing. He and Joseph agreed that he'd keep talking and Joseph would keep listening.

Petricia hung onto Joseph's shirttail while Jones and the other warriors kept their railguns aimed to the sides.

There are none from the local Pod around. This tunnel appears to have been used recently, but I cannot tell you where they have gone.

Up short slopes, down slope around corners, through fallen rocks, and still they kept going. Progress was slow and Bundin's idea of 'nearby' seemed far different from Joseph's.

The rocket explosions and impacts of the mechs directly overhead shook the tunnel. Joseph knew they were close to the complex, close to the underground facility. They stopped briefly to cover their heads as small rocks and dust filled the air around them.

One more turn of the tunnel and Bundin appeared, blue in the muted white light. The eyes on his stalk blinked rapidly when the bright beam washed over him.

"Sorry about that," Joseph apologized.

The tunnel was not much wider than the Podder. Joseph worked his way past first, followed closely by Petricia. Two warriors stayed behind and two moved in front of Bundin where the tunnel continued into the distance, disappearing around a corner after twenty meters.

Joseph looked at the door, trying to discern how to open it. There was no handle, no lock, no hinges, and no access pad of any sort. It was a blank door, little more than a metal wall in the middle of a rock tunnel.

Petricia leaned back against the Podder's shell and crossed her arms as she tried to relax. She found the confines of the tunnel pressing in with her only relief coming when she focused on Joseph and what he was doing. She stared at him as he meticulously searched the door and the area around it.

Jones tiptoed to the corner and looked around it. He couldn't see anything. He listened intently, but heard nothing. He stayed where he was, railgun aimed into the darkness.

Joseph used his small knife to pry into the gaps, but could find no purchase. The door refused to budge.

"If you told me that this was not a door, I would believe you," he said to Petricia as he joined her in leaning against Bundin's shell.

A single blast shook the door. More dust drifted through the air.

Joseph rotated his railgun from his back and aimed at

the door. "Take cover, boys," he told them. Bundin backed up and Petricia stood behind him. Jones and the second warrior disappeared around the bend in the tunnel ahead.

Joseph fired at the sides, but the hypervelocity darts didn't penetrate. He only needed to fire twice to learn that shattering projectiles within a closed space was a bad idea.

The metal is only as strong as the rock within which it is set, Bundin thought.

"Fire in the hole," Joseph said as he aimed a second time, but this time at the rock to the side of the doorway.

The cracks boomed within the tunnel, echoing into the distance. The dust danced with each new shot. But the rock was giving way. Chips were flying from around the casement. When it was all exposed, Joseph stopped firing. He let go of his rifle, and the combat sling let it flop to his side. He jammed his fingers into the gap he'd created and found the other side of the door frame. He dug his fingers in and pulled until he could brace his feet on the wall and then with all his Vampiric strength, he ripped the casement out and the doorway fell to the tunnel floor.

Beyond, he saw a well-lit space that appeared to be a luxury bathroom.

23

The *War Axe*

"Captain San Marino, how are you?" Auburn's dark skin glistened with the odd lighting inside the drop ship.

"I'm fine, and would love to catch up, but I expect this isn't a social call," Micky replied.

"Colonel Walton asked me to contact you and let you know that we're working to get inside the Crenellian headquarters. If there's a problem and they launched their weapons against the planet, we're going to need a pick up. Can you be here in four hours?"

Micky's face dropped. "I cannot. We've been slowing down, but we are still heading away from Tissikinnon Four. I thought we might have another day before we needed to start the process to return to the planet. Do we know if the orbital defenses have been neutralized?"

"Not by us they haven't, not yet anyway," Auburn replied.

"I have to get us turned around and heading that way.

Smedley will provide an update as soon as we have it. Tell Terry that we're on our way at the best possible speed."

"Will do, Skipper," Auburn said, using Terry's name for the captain.

Micky liked it, continuing to look at the screen long after Auburn had signed off.

"Helm, turn us around right freaking now. They need us on Tissikinnon Four."

Clifton gave the thumbs up over his shoulder as he started entering commands. "Changing the heading now."

Micky didn't feel anything as the ship turned to face the planet as it continued on a trajectory away from the planet. In space, aerodynamics were mostly irrelevant. The ship was flying backwards, but that ability solved the problem of how to reverse a space drive.

Don't. Turn the ship and always accelerate in one direction.

"If you could inform the crew to strap in, Captain, I'd appreciate it. They're going to feel a little bump..."

PODDERN

Terry, Char, and Kaeden inspected the damage to the door leading underground. The surface was scorched and chipped, but when Kae leveraged the strength of his powered armor against the door, it wouldn't budge.

"Doesn't that suck a whole bunch," Char said.

Terry looked at the hatch and pulled his Jean Dukes Special. He flipped it over to eleven with his thumb. "It goes to eleven," he said in a low voice.

"Embrace the suck, Dad!" Kae called.

"But not yet," Terry replied and put his weapon away. "Once the mechs are recharged, you think four of them pulling together might get this thing open?"

"Won't know until we try." Kae looked disappointed.

"Can't do it." Terry gripped his son's armored hand. "Not yet anyway. If we kill them and their equipment, then we condemn the planet. Let's not be in a hurry to do that."

"Has anyone heard from Joseph lately?" Char asked.

JOSEPH AND PETRICIA LOOKED INSIDE. It appeared to be an empty bathroom. Jones appeared beside them.

"Let us go in first," Jones suggested.

"As you wish." Joseph stepped aside. Jones and the second warrior rushed in, jumping to the sides and covering each other with the bounding overwatch technique. Joseph and Petricia walked in. Joseph reached out with his telepathic mind.

"A dozen Crenellians in the room beyond," Joseph whispered, raising his railgun and making sure that Petricia stayed behind him.

Bundin worked his way through the opening and stopped within the bathroom. He looked from one fixture to the next. None of it made any sense to him. Jones and Einar stood at the door that led out of the bathroom, counting down on their fingers. At zero, Einar yanked the door open and Jones ran through.

"DOWN ON THE FLOOR!" Jones yelled. Joseph waved Einar through in front of him. The warrior ran past Jones to occupy a flanking position overlooking the Crenellians seated before two long banks of computers.

The room was large at twenty meters per side. There were two rows of computers, more systems than aliens. None of the Crenellians had moved.

Joseph walked in, touching Jones gently on the arm as he walked by. "My name is Joseph and I'm with the Bad Company. Your president hired us to end this war and we intend to do just that, but we need your help to do that."

Petricia walked up behind Joseph and waited.

"That looks like the tunnel out," Joseph pointed. "Would you mind terribly opening the door for our friends and fellows?"

Petricia walked past the Crenellians. Some watched her, others seemed indifferent, but when the Podder came into view, their attention snapped to the alien with the blue shell and stalk-head.

Jones and Einar eyed the small humanoids warily as Petricia continued up the tunnel. She knew there was fresh air on the other side and that hastened her steps. She'd had enough of being underground.

The door was more like a hatch, massive in construction but angled to keep people out. She cycled the unlock mechanism and tapped a lever that led to a counterweight. It dropped and the door cranked open. As it popped, she closed her eyes and took a deep breath. She smelled sulfur and explosive, but it was still outside air.

When she opened her eyes, she found railgun barrels pointed at her, one from a mech, and pistols from both Terry Henry and Char.

"It's Petricia," she said weakly.

"At ease!" Terry called. "You can't imagine how much grief you just saved us."

Petricia nodded and started to climb the stairs out as the door was over her head. Terry was climbing in and ran into her. She pointed outside. Terry stepped back.

"Tunnels not your speed?" he asked.

"Not in the least," she said with a half-smile. Char helped her out and she looked back.

"We'll tell Joseph," Terry said. Being underground wasn't natural. He thought a vampire would take to it better, but Petricia had always been different. "Kae, get Auburn in here with our comm gear. I want Smedley knee-deep in this shit in five, and where are the rest of my Crooners? Get them in here, too!"

TERRY CLIMBED down the stairs and strode down the tunnel. Char was right beside him as they walked into the Crenellian planetary command center.

When he arrived, he found Joseph holding out his hands as three of the small humanoids were chittering at Bundin, who was wildly waving his tentacle arms.

"SHUT UP!" Terry bellowed, wading into the small aliens and bouncing them aside. "You stop!" Terry pointed to Bundin. "And you sit the fuck down!"

The Crenellians stood their ground. Terry grabbed one in each hand and slammed them into their seats. Char picked up the third and dumped him into the nearest empty chair.

Terry looked at the workstations. "Check the bunk

room," Terry said, pointing to a third door. "That one will be the kitchen. Should be some sleepers in there. Wake them up and drag them out here."

Terry turned back to the aliens. The Podder continued to wave his arms.

"Can you calm him down, please?" Terry asked Joseph, who worked to get Bundin through the door and into the bathroom. He shut the door once they were through.

"Which one of you is in charge?" Terry stood with his hands on his hips and waited. No one spoke up. The pitter patter of little feet signaled the arrival of the other nine Crenellians. Jones and Einar chased twelve out of the bunk room. At least they looked tired instead of arrogant.

"Come on now. One of you goofy bastards is in charge." Terry waited as the group was herded together. "Tik'Po'Rout, talk with them please and let them know that we are deadly serious."

The small alien stepped forward. "They are deadly serious," he said.

"I haven't killed a Crooner, but I'm about to start, until I find one that's halfway decent."

Char moved closer to her husband to keep him from flying into a rage. "Joseph," she said casually. "We could use your assistance in here."

Down the tunnel, the werewolves, weretigers, and Pricolici trotted to join their fellows during the interrogation of the Crenellians.

"I'm Colonel Terry Henry Walton, leader of the Bad Company's Direct Action Branch. We have been hired by your president to end this war. We're going to do exactly that. The next piece in this puzzle involves you shutting down your weaponry, so I need you to jump onto your system and start turning things off."

The assembled group of small aliens looked at him with no hint of any desire to take action.

"Ankh, can you please tell them that we are going to do this? There's only one scenario where the Crenellians survive, and that depends completely on their cooperation."

Ankh'Po'Turn hesitated briefly, looking at Terry with a blank expression before turning to one of the Crenellians. "Do as he tells you or he will destroy your computers and then abandon you outside, or worse, in the tunnels with only Tiskers for company."

"I don't understand," the alien replied. "They were hired by our president so what are they doing here, destroying our equipment and threatening us?" The small humanoid waved in the direction of the tunnel and then back to the computers.

Terry was surprised by the emotion shown. It took destroying three computers before the last group came out of their shells. Terry appreciated Ankh's improvisation. The colonel hadn't mentioned abandoning the Crooners outside or in the tunnels, but that was something they didn't know they feared.

Auburn appeared and started setting up the equipment. Joseph opened the door from the bathroom and walked in, slowly closing the door behind himself.

"My boys are with Bundin. He's better now that he doesn't have to look at this bunch," Joseph whispered into Terry's ear from behind.

"I wish I didn't have to look at this bunch," Terry whispered out the side of his mouth. "Can you get a login from that one and turn on the computer, please? We'll let Smedley do it. I'm not feeling the love from these guys."

Joseph walked past Terry, looked at the Crenellian that Ankh had talked with, and then continued to the nearest terminal. With a few screen taps, the system came on.

"Smedley, do your thing," Terry said before waving an arm at the Crenellians. "Get them out of here, all except Ankh and that one."

The one whose mind Joseph had pulled the login code from.

"What's your name?" Terry asked once the warriors had herded the others up the tunnel. There was shouting at the entrance as Kimber and the platoon took charge of the small humanoid aliens.

"Don't hurt any of them!" Terry yelled toward the tunnel before turning to face the Crenellian leader. "I asked your name."

The humanoid looked at him with the expression that he loathed—one of complete indifference.

"I'm in, Colonel Walton," Smedley said happily. "Oh, my."

Terry looked at the communications equipment. That wasn't an expression he had wanted to hear. "Oh, my?"

"This interface is different. It has access to everything, but we need the master code."

"Standby, General." Terry physically turned the alien so he was facing the screen. "What's the code?"

Joseph nodded and started tapping.

"Thank you, Colonel Walton," Smedley said before continuing. The screen in front of Joseph started flashing as the EI took over. "I'm deactivating the orbital defenses. There are two other ground assault systems that had been turned loose. I'm deactivating those now. I'm removing the access from the four remaining Crenellian outposts. Done and done."

"Why would you do that?" the alien leader asked.

Terry took a knee so he could look the man in the face. "Because we can't have a conversation while weapons are pointed in people's faces."

"But that's what you did," he countered.

"We didn't shoot any of your people. Our failsafe is no harm. If we die, we don't wipe out all life on the planet. Because of the threat of your force, we had to use force of our own. It's not logical, but it is human. The Crenellian president hired us to do a job and then the Crenellians actively worked against us. You tell me how that makes sense? We were supposed to stop a war, not participate in a genocide."

"They are only Tiskers," he replied.

Terry clenched his jaw. "Get him out of here," Terry growled.

Hidden in a remote corner of the Pan Galaxy

Nathan Lowell leaned back in his office chair. Ecaterina sat across from him.

"What do you think of the Direct Action Branch?" she asked.

"We set Terry Henry up poorly on his first mission, but he's taking care of business. I hate to say it, but we did the same thing to Valerie too, but she's handling things quite nicely as well. It confirms the old saying that you don't have to be great, but you need to be surrounded by great people. I think we've done that."

"I think so, too," she replied, looking uncomfortable. Nathan knew why she was unhappy.

"Christina is doing fine. Better than fine, but the Tissikinnon action is ongoing. I hope Terry resolves it sometime soon so she can call us from the *War Axe*. I miss my little girl," Nathan added.

Ecaterina nodded, her eyes glistening as she fought off

the tears. Christina had been an adult for a long time, but she never stopped being their only child.

Nathan stared at his computer screen as if willing it to connect. "Screw it," he said before tilting his head back in his take-charge pose. "Activate a comm channel directly to Terry Henry Walton."

The screen came to life showing Terry up close, but he was looking at something off-screen. Behind him, Nathan and Ecaterina could make out banks of computers.

"You are the fucking man, Smedley!" Terry hooted. "Goddamn, you showed this system who's boss. Fuck that little piece of shit. YES!" Terry stood up and started dancing the pelvic thrust.

"TH?" Nathan interrupted.

Terry looked at the screen. "Stop fucking with me, Smedley. Why did you put on a Nathan Lowell mask? Is it Halloween? With all the aliens out here, what do people dress up as? It boggles the mind, don't you think?"

"It *is* Nathan, Terry. Are you okay?"

"Whoa! How'd you get in there?" Terry sat down and assumed a contemplative yet executive pose. "What can I do for you, Nathan? Hi, Ecaterina. I didn't see you standing there."

"We were talking and figured you were in the final stages of the operation, so instead of speculating on your status, we called. Was that your victory dance, TH?" Nathan asked.

"That was my not-safe-for-work-or-public-consumption dance. We have disabled all the automated scorched-earth systems the Crenellians installed here. The next step is to talk with the Podders and come to a new agreement. I have no estimate for how long that will take, but at least no one is dying anymore." Terry looked down, furled his brow, and then looked back up. "I lost one, Nathan, and a second lost her leg, but she's on the mend."

"I'm sorry to hear that, TH. Please accept my condolences."

"We went into this with our eyes wide open, Nathan. It's nothing *you* did. I only want to make sure that our next job isn't a veiled attempt by one race to cleanse another from existence."

"Is that what they really wanted?"

"They wanted the Podders to help them with the mining, but my impression is that they never were able to communicate fully with the locals, plus there's no single Podder government. Every region is different. What they negotiated and however they negotiated it didn't apply to where they sunk their first shafts. With Joseph's help, we're able to talk to at least one Pod. If they agree to restore the original conditions, the Crenellians will get their minerals and the Podders will get whatever they expected from the bargain, which might be Bad Company's protection from the galaxy's predators. Can I agree to give them that?"

"It wouldn't be the Bad Company, but we could sign a pact on behalf of the Force de Guerre, an official Federation agency. Kurtz is doing a good job getting it set up. For any signed documents, have Colonel Marcie Walton's name as the nominal head of the FDG. We need to keep you separate."

"That's good to hear on Kurtz and the FDG, Nathan. We'll make sure we get it right. Anything else?" Terry asked.

"Christina?"

"Christina is doing great. A valuable member of the team. She is uninjured and helping the others. She seems to work well with the weretigers. On a side note, if I wanted to recruit a Podder to the team, can I do that?"

"Can we talk with her?" Ecaterina asked.

"I'm sorry, Ecaterina, but she's topside. I'm finishing things up here in the Crooner control room." Terry held his ear out and listened intently. "It's quiet as can be up there. I expect they're taking some well-earned downtime."

"I'm glad Christina has found a home with people who care about her," Nathan replied, smiling at Ecaterina. "You can recruit whoever you want for the company. Just understand the logistics support aliens will need. You know what they say, amateurs talk tactics, professionals talk logistics."

"Hey! I taught you that," Terry said as Nathan's image faded.

GENERAL SMEDLEY BUTLER reappeared on the screen. "Smedley! Tell the captain that orbital defenses have been disabled."

"Already done, Colonel. We'll be scooping up what remains of the system for further analysis. Both hangar bay doors are operational and we look forward to your return to the ship."

"Sounds great. Thaw some steaks for my people. They deserve it. And change the access codes on this system or whatever you need to do to prevent any Crooners from reactivating the failsafe."

"That also has already been done."

"You are the bomb, Smedley. Walton out." Terry shut down the comm system. He stood and stretched before going to the bathroom door where he found Bundin and the two warriors. "Come on, we're leaving, and we have a mission for you, buddy."

They worked their way through the control room and out the tunnel.

Once outside and with the inner circle gathered with all the Were in their human forms, Terry turned to Joseph.

"Good job getting this far, my friends. The next part could be the hardest or the easiest. Joseph, I'd like Bundin to meet with his Pod and see if a conversation is possible between them and the Crooners. If so, we'll bring the team and let the negotiations happen. I'll act as a mediator so the Crooners will be accepting of whatever I tell them is fair."

"We have to emphasize what the Crenellians want and how it is delivered," Char suggested.

"Kimber, bring that Crenellian leader in here and see if Ankh will come, too."

Kimber nodded and walked toward her platoon that was spread out, half of them asleep while the other half guarded the Crenellians.

"Are they prisoners of war?" Timmons asked.

"In the pre-WWDE sense of the word? No. They are detainees. We are securing their safety by taking away their liberty. What a deal for them!" Terry smiled and shook his head. "We'll turn them loose as soon as we can, as soon as their people can come pick them up."

Kimber was carrying the alien leader while Ankh walked by her side.

"Thank you for coming, Ankh, and you too, whatever your name is. I need to know what the original agreement between Crenellia and Tissikinnon Four was all about. What did you get from the deal?"

The leader stared at Bundin. Joseph started to laugh but stifled it quickly. Terry rolled his eyes, but appreciated the bond Joseph and the Podder had formed that they could joke at the Crenellian's expense.

"Dammit! Auburn, can you set us up so Smedley can join us?"

Char handed Terry her comm device. "Smedley, have you been able to find the original agreement between the Podders and the Crenellians?"

"Yes. It was for monthly deliveries of four elements that are common on Tissikinnon Four but rare on Crenellia."

"Joseph, can you translate the elements and monthly quantities for Bundin? The billion-credit question. What would the Podders want to deliver that amount to the surface monthly for the Crenellians to pick up?"

Joseph nodded and leaned on Bundin's shell as they conversed, silently, mind to mind. The vampire had found that by touching the Podder, they could speak clearly to each other.

"Do you think he would fit in a Pod Doc?" Terry asked Char. She leaned one way and then another.

"Maybe," was the most to which she would commit.

Dokken sighed. The German Shepherd was exhausted, but his cat naps weren't doing it. He needed a good sleep on a bed. *When are we leaving?* he asked.

Only as soon as humanly possible, Terry replied, scratching the dog behind his ears.

The wait grew long and Terry started to look for a place to sit. Half of the others had already dropped to the ground, their exhaustion near complete. The more that Terry and Char did nothing, the more the fatigue gripped them.

Petricia seemed to be asleep on her feet as she draped herself across Bundin's shell, leaning against Joseph.

Christina started to snore. The Crenellians looked at her oddly.

"What is that noise?" Ankh asked.

Marcie strolled up. Terry and Char hadn't seen her leave. A towel was over her shoulders and her hair was still wet.

"What?" she asked.

Char's mouth dropped open. "I've been out here wallowing in my own filth while you're in there taking a shower?"

"Yes," Marcie replied matter-of-factly.

Char smiled and bolted for the doorway. Snoring with one breath and awake with the next, Christina popped upright. "Showers?" she said. "That's right!"

Before Terry could say anything, she was running toward the tunnel, too.

Joseph stepped away from Bundin. "He says it is no problem at all. What they want in return is a food facility, as long as Terry Henry Walton's Bad Company will provide security. The Podder foray into arming themselves has been a disaster. They won't seek to do it again."

"Can Bundin speak for his people? What about the blue Podders?" Terry said, using their terminology. He couldn't tell them apart and wouldn't try.

"Bundin suspects that the attack by the behemoth tank eliminated the blue Pod."

"Eliminated?" Terry said, noticing the look of despair that flashed across Kae's face.

"Yes. They marched to their deaths against the tank. When a Pod commits, every member of that Pod commits. The problem with the initial attack on the Crenellians was that it wasn't the original Pod that made the agreement, but once that Pod saw the Crenellians attacking, they responded in kind, including attacking us when we appeared in the middle of it all."

"Will they continue to attack us?"

"No. Bundin assures me that after he talks with them, we will be friends of the Pod."

"You know what, Joseph?" Terry asked.

The vampire shook his head.

"I think I'm going to join my wife. Well done, Joseph. Really well done. We could not have pulled this off without you," Terry tipped his chin to the vampire. "Or you—" Pointing to Bundin. "—or you—" Pointing to Kaeden. "—or you—" To Marcie, before taking the rest in with a wave of his arm. "Or all of you. No one fights alone. No one dies alone. No one is forgotten. Here's to Xandrie and Adams, the first Were members of the FDG to fall, and here's to Cantor, the latest to give his life in bringing justice to the universe."

The others raised their fists as a sign of strength. Terry looked on them with pride, eyes glistening as he turned and headed for the tunnel.

"You better not be getting naked down there," Kim said into the silence.

Shortly thereafter, Christina appeared in the doorway to the tunnel entrance, hair still dripping. "I had to leave. There was all kinds of crazy going on down there."

THE BAD COMPANY was getting ready to leave. Instead of waiting until the morning, they were packing up. Everyone was tired to the point of exhaustion.

Three drop ships were lined up in the killing field before the destroyed defenses of the Crenellian headquarters. Had the company made it that close before the weapon systems opened up, no one would have escaped alive.

Joseph, Petricia, and Bundin had taken the fourth ship to the area controlled by his Pod to start the negotiations.

Eight armored suits had nominal power and two new volunteers manned Cantor's and Fleeter's. Kae was pleased that a number of warriors had stepped up.

He wondered at what point the entire company would be mechanized. The suits had made a difference in this conflict. The only one to die had been a mech driver, but while he was outside of his suit at the time. There was much they learned and more to incorporate before their next engagement. Kae had a great deal of work to do, including delivering a fitting eulogy.

Owing to the big door and wide tunnel, the mechs had been a valuable asset in removing all the equipment from the Crenellian headquarters. The small humanoids finally showed emotion as their computers were separated and piled inside the shuttles.

"What happens to us?" Ankh asked.

"You are the only one who seems capable of looking at the big picture. What makes you different and how can we get some of these others to see things that way? It is how the universe works," Terry explained.

"They consider me a radical." The small alien never bowed his head or shoulders. He showed no emotion at all.

"In my experience, Ankh, those are the ones who change the world, for both good and bad. But your help has saved lives. I think we could use you as a liaison between the Bad Company and the Crenellian government. Heaven knows that I can't be trusted to talk with your president."

"You want me to talk with my president? But I'm not in his class," Ankh argued.

"Who cares when you graduated?" Terry replied.

"What? He is in a different social class. I am a technician, as are all of us on the Tissikinnon mission. The upper class never leave Crenellia."

"Maybe it's time they got out to see the galaxy. It's a beautiful place out here, Ankh."

The lights from the mechs and the shuttles cut through the darkness, but the desolation of the area wasn't very inviting. The constant overcast skies blocked the stars.

"Not so much," Ankh offered.

"Maybe not right here, but there's a lot more out there. A whole universe, my small friend."

"I will consider it," Ankh said, not changing his expression.

"Tell the others that we've sent a message to your president that we will drop you off at Federation Frontier

Station Seven, the first gate from this area of space. Your people will be picked up from there, but I expect some of the Federation's sharpest minds from our research and development group would like to talk with you, too. The Crenellians remind me of a good friend of mine. I think you guys would get along famously with him, outside of the Crenellian proclivity toward genocide, that is."

Etheric Empire Research Facility on R2D2

"What am I to do with you," Felicity drawled. Ted didn't ignore her. He'd shut out the rest of the world as he focused on the miniaturization and manufacture optimization of gate drive technology.

She knew that he'd become completely absorbed. The R&D station was not designed for any social life because it was built by people just like Ted whose work was paramount to their lives.

Felicity put a hand on her husband's arm, surprising him. "You haven't been back to our quarters for two days now. You need to eat and you need to sleep. Remember our deal!" she said forcefully, the only way she'd been able to break Ted out of his complete immersion into his projects.

"Yes. Yes. I know," he replied with a dismissive wave before turning back to his computer. She didn't let him. Felicity turned him toward her, making him face her as she held him by the shoulders.

"Ted, if we don't get off this station, I will die," she said.

He smirked. "Don't be so dramatic. Everything you need is here. Everything *I* need is here," Ted said slowly, as he did when trying to explain things to his wife.

She knew why he did that. He thought of her as intellectually inferior. She admitted that she didn't understand the engineering and physics that he lovingly embraced. She knew that he was a true genius, gifted beyond measure, as well as a werewolf, though he hadn't changed into Were form in decades, maybe even a century or longer.

As long as they'd been together.

"I miss our children," she told him. Ted was capable of shutting everything and everyone out of his life, except for his children. When the topic came up, he would put aside what he was doing and pay attention.

"I do, too. One of the other teams is working on a comm link to improve how we can talk with Earth. I will make sure that our kids get one of the comm units so you can talk with them whenever you want."

"I get lonely," Felicity said softly.

The comm unit buzzed. Ted looked at it oddly. "Lance Reynolds?"

"Good morning, Ted, maybe evening. I don't know how things translate to where you are. Glad to see you're up, regardless. Your unit is being reassigned so you get better security for your work. I hope you don't mind, but I'm putting you on Keeg Station in the Dren Cluster. They have full facilities."

"Hi, Lance. You are looking as marvelous as ever," Felicity drawled. "Isn't that where the Bad Company is located?"

"Only the Direct Action Branch of the Bad Company. You'll be co-located with Terry and his people."

Felicity closed her eyes and smiled. "Do they have shops on Keeg Station and a reason to wear nice clothes?"

"They need a station manager, someone who has experience...say, a former mayor for example," the general replied with a smile. "Would you know anyone like that?"

Ted looked at the screen. "Felicity used to be mayor back in North Chicago," Ted said as if making a revelation on behalf of his wife.

"Pack your bags. The ship will pick you up today," the general said. "Reynolds out."

Ted looked at the blank screen. "But he didn't ask where I was on my research. I wanted to tell him that I'm getting closer."

"Of course, Ted dear. We'll call him back and let him know as soon as we're packed and on the next ship to our new home with our old friends."

PODDERN

They were still loading the drop ships when Joseph returned. Terry and Char stopped what they were doing. Her helmet was off while her hair dried.

The shuttle landed and the rear ramp dropped. Bundin was the first one out, followed by Joseph and Petricia.

"They'll have the first shipment ready in two weeks," Joseph said proudly.

"And from the Crenellian end?"

"They want grass seed and cattle. I gave them some of my beef jerky to try. They were over the moon. So they want to raise their own cattle or bistok. Instead of the Crenellians providing food, the Podders want a means of growing the food themselves."

Dokken panted with his mouth open at the mention of beef jerky. Everyone nearby held up their hands. They were out.

"Poor puppy. No hot meals on this objective," Kae said from his armored suit, reiterating TH's old joke about always telling the troops that there would be hot chow on the objective, whether there would be or not.

No shit, Dokken replied.

"And Bundin?" Terry asked.

"He was hoping to be the first of his people to leave the planet. He's already a legend for stopping the war."

"Bundin took all the credit?"

"That was my recommendation. For ending the civil war and finishing the Crenellians. He said it made him popular with the ladies."

"What the hell is that? And don't tell me. The way you can tell the women from the men is that they're blue."

"Well, yeah…"

ON BOARD the *War Axe*

Micky thought the ship had exceeded its performance limits on the return trip. They had accelerated faster than they were supposedly capable of and stopped in such a short distance that he thought the sail, the area where the bridge was located, should have been ripped from the ship.

He wondered if Clifton, Smedley, and Suresha had been

toying with things, but would check the data when he had time.

The recovery of Terry and his people had gone smoothly. When the *War Axe* arrived, they sent down the other two shuttles with Smedley flying them and no one aboard as Terry had said he was bringing a bunch of aliens and confiscated equipment back to the ship.

While the *War Axe* waited in orbit, the structures and stores departments collected as much debris and intact gear as they could from the Crenellian orbital defense system that they'd attacked on their last pass.

They were able to half-fill the hangar bay with mines, two intact fighters, and pieces of the buoy.

Once the shuttles were back aboard, they'd unloaded quickly. Micky had also noted that they'd taken one body bag to the ship's morgue and one person on a stretcher straight to the Pod Doc. He wondered if every mission was going to be like that.

A blue stalk-headed alien was roaming the corridors in the company of the vampires. A small humanoid alien was doing the same thing, but he was being escorted by Marcie and Kaeden. The other fifty Crenellians they'd pulled from all the outposts were given an excess berthing space where they sat nearly catatonic.

Company warriors stood guard because the group was strictly prohibited from accessing the ship's computer systems.

"We need to figure out a way to keep them occupied," Micky said as much to himself as the company in his briefing room.

Terry's head hung as he sat at the conference table. Micky didn't know if he was awake or not. Char sat up straight, but her eyes were closed and her mouth hung slack as she was out cold.

The captain watched them briefly, believing that they hadn't slept for the entire time they'd been on the planet.

"Smedley, activate the comm system and link us through, please."

Nathan appeared and gave Captain Micky San Marino a hearty good morning. Micky smiled and pointed the camera at the leaders of the Bad Company's Direct Action Branch. Nathan watched them, shaking his head.

Micky got up and walked behind the two, putting his hands gently on their shoulders. Terry about came out of his skin, making the captain jump back, stumble, and slam into the wall.

Terry mumbled an apology before blinking the hologram into focus. "Oh! Hi, Nathan. How's it hanging?"

"You've looked better, TH. Although Char is spectacular as always. I don't know why she strapped herself to a goon like you."

The whites of Char's eyes showed round as she forced her eyes open, making her look like a zombie.

Which was *exactly* how she felt.

Terry turned his head, saw her vacant expression, and started to chuckle.

"You have a way with words," Terry started, before taking a deep breath and repeating the report that he'd prepared in his head.

After two minutes, Nathan stopped him.

"You know who Ronald Reagan was. Remember when he asked for the entire budget of the United States to be condensed down to one page? Give me that version."

"We ended the war and we made more than we spent. We acquired a Podder and a Crooner for the team. They bring unique capabilities, diversity, strength of mind and character, all of that. I don't think we'll be misled again into fighting some knucklehead's war for him. Were you able to talk with dickface?"

"You mean the president?" Nathan asked, knowing exactly what Terry Henry meant.

The colonel nodded. Nathan leaned close to his monitor. Char hadn't blinked. He was convinced that she was sound asleep with her eyes wide open. He looked back to Terry.

"Yes. He's pleased with the outcome and delivered an abject apology. He said that he wasn't deliberately misleading. I don't believe him, but we have our money in hand including the bonus and kicker. Your first mission and you are well on your way to paying off the *War Axe*. Only another three hundred and seven like that and you'll own it outright."

"Say what?" Terry raised one eyebrow.

Nathan maintained a dead-pan expression. "Just keep plugging away and you'll be living the good life, retired on a Caribbean island."

"Already did that. It's exhausting." Terry rubbed the stubble on his face. "I need to put this one to bed." He pointed to Char. "And then check on my people. You know the status—one lost, one severely injured."

"General Reynolds has sent Ted and a research group from R2D2 to Keeg Station for security reasons. We've received too much intel that suggests the facility is a prime target for undesirables. Ted seemed indifferent, but Felicity was ecstatic, or so I hear. She's also going to be the station manager. The last one died in a bar fight with an Asplesian."

"What's an Asplesian?" Terry mumbled.

"You'll find out. I'm sure Felicity won't put up with any of their crap."

"The old team, back together already. I like it. I'm sure Ted and our Crooner will get along like old buds," Terry suggested.

"It looks to me like warfighting suits you, TH." Nathan waved a handful of papers in front of the camera. "I've sent a batch of RFPs, requests for proposals, your way. Take a look and see what grabs you. They all need the Bad Company yesterday."

Nathan and Terry both shook their heads as they looked at the image of the other.

"Will do, when I can see to read the words, Nathan. All I have to say is fuck those guys, and fuck the next bunch too, whoever they may be."

"Truer words were never spoken. Until then, Terry Henry. Thank you for a job well done."

The End of The Bad Company
Don't stop now! Keep turning the pages as Craig & Michael talk about their thoughts on this book and the overall project called the Age of Expansion (and if you

haven't read the ten-book prequel, the Terry Henry Walton Chronicles, now is a great time to take a look).
Terry, Char, and the rest of the Bad Company's Direct Action Branch will return in Bad Company Book 2 - Blockade.

Welcome to the Age of Expansion

Thank you for reading beyond the end of the book and all the way to the author notes. You are the bomb!

If you join my mailing list, you'll get notified on release day for every new book in this series, and **every new book is only 99 cents on release day**, as a reward for those who are on my newsletter list and follow me on Facebook. Thank you very much for coming on board. There are so many stories left to tell.

If this is your first foray into the world of Terry Henry Walton, we have some news. There's about ¾ of a million words of other Terry Henry & Charumati stories out there. Always free in Kindle Unlimited – binge read to your heart's content. And then there's the series that spawned the Terry Henry Walton Chronicles – the brainchild of master storyteller, Michael Anderle, the Kurtherian Gambit. Check those books out – twenty one in the main series and four in the Second Dark Ages companion series.

Do you wonder how it all started? Let me tell you a story.

I was active in Michael's Facebook group 20book-sto50k that is all about helping authors understand the business and then realize their dreams. Here's an email he sent to me on October 12, 2016 (way back when).

Craig:

In books 12 and 13, I have a character (ex-military, mercenary - good-ish guy) that I'm thinking is going to stay on earth instead of going with team(s) due to relationship with a Professor that is also in the stories.

If you are willing, we can talk about whether he is a good character to use for your series as some fans are wanting to know what happens with him. My thought, if you concur, is to juice him up a little for his support of TQB which would allow him to last through the time (spruce him back up and give him enough that he should 'last' to 120 - same with her ...But, she will die of course) ... Plus, Akio would know him (or at least remember him).

He has a certain level of 'what's in it for me' attitude that would fit our story discussions last week.

Not sure how to go from here on the idea... I can pull his chapters maybe? Or just download books 12 and 13 and look for 'Terry' (the guy) and read those sections?

Michael.

Simple as that. I received Michael's email on October 12th of 2016. I didn't start writing Terry Henry Walton until after Thanksgiving that year. The "her" was Melissa and in order to make Terry Henry a little jaded, that character was murdered on the world's worst day ever (WWDE) and we introduced the Werewolf Charumati as a character who would stand the test of time and be long enough lived to keep TH company. Char is about twenty-five years older than Terry.

On October 12th, 2017, one year after Michael's email, we published Gateway to the Universe, the thirteenth book that Michael and I collaborated on, putting us just under 800,000 total words about Terry, Char, and humanity's return to civilization. With this book, we are where I wanted to finally get to – military science fiction and space opera. I love this stuff. I enjoyed writing Terry & Char on a post-apocalyptic Earth, but in space? There are so many more story lines.

Is Terry a good-ish guy? You can judge for yourself.

Michael contacted me because I'd written a best-selling post-apocalyptic series with the End Times Alaska, I spent twenty years in the Marine Corps, and I'm married to a professor. Seems like Michael wrote Terry Henry Walton just for me. He didn't, but that's the story I'll tell my grandchildren.

And then there are the other spin-offs.

My writing partner in this endeavor is a dynamo when it comes to the self-publishing universe. He has created something wonderful to feed a loyal readership the highest quality stories in a universe that they're comfortable with. Michael makes magic happen.

We say that we write pulp, but it's better than that. These aren't hollow words. We strive to make each sentence better than the last. And we have the best beta readers in the world. I run short bits by a subset of the Just In Time team and people that I trust to give me feedback that validates my approach while making recommendations to make the story better. I still have to write the story, but they hold me to a high standard.

Shout out to Micky Cocker (I named the captain of the *War Axe* in her honor – he will be prominent in all the Bad Company books), James Caplan (the mech driver Capples), Kelly O'Donnell (the mech driver Kelly), Diane Velasquez, and Dorene Johnson. If nothing else, pleasing these five with my stories means success – they provide a great cross-section of experience and perspective. Di & Do, the Double Ds as they are known, are my developmental editors. They tolerate getting odd chapters at odd times with questions like, "Does this work for a transition to a more mature character?" or "How is the pace so far?"

I needed more names for The Bad Company, so I trolled a few feeds, and found on my future collaborator Tommy Dublin's site a cousin from Ireland, so we have adopted Clodagh Shortall as an engineering assistant who has been found to be secretly harboring the good king Wenceslaus, our favorite orange cat and arch-enemy of our favorite dog.

I also borrowed from J (Jim) Clifton Slater, an old Marine veteran who was incredibly helpful with the 20Books Vegas authors conference that I run. I could not have done it without him, so Clifton gets to fly the *War Axe*.

And I still live in the Sub-Arctic.

As winter approaches, I've had to get all kinds of things ready – the snow blower on the front of my tractor, the walk behind snow blower, clean up the outside stuff, and brace for impact. When winter hits, it can get pretty intense this close to the Arctic Circle. I live outside Fairbanks, Alaska which means the darkness is coming. We have about 3 ½ hours of daylight on the winter solstice.

That means prime writing time. It's cold and dark, but not in my office. Phyllis the Arctic Dog, our pit bull prefers temperatures from 20F to 40F. Warmer than that and she pants like it is mid-summer. Colder than that and we have to wrestle her boots on. At -20F she gets very efficient, spending about 30 seconds to a minute outside to take care of business. In the summer, she'll take 30 to 45 minutes to go. I don't blame her – we have nice property and a healthy-sized forest behind our house where we hang out.

I bought a truck (2015 Nissan Titan) since last winter. I have high hopes that this will make a great winter truck. It is heavy enough that I should maintain traction. I'm going with the Toyo winter tires as opposed to Blizzak for it. The place that sells the Blizzaks rubbed me the wrong way so they won't be getting my business. Easy enough – I'll let my money do the talking. And now that I have the Toyo tires on, the truck drives like a tank in the snow and ice. I am quite pleased.

That's it – break's over, back to writing the next book. Peace, fellow humans.

Please join my Newsletter (www.craigmartelle.com – please, please, please sign up!), or you can follow me on Facebook since you'll get the same opportunity to pick up the books for only 99 cents on that first day they are published.

If you liked this story, you might like some of my other books. You can join my mailing list by dropping by my website **www.craigmartelle.com** or if you have any comments, shoot me a note at craig@craigmartelle.com. I am always happy to hear from people who've read my work. I try to answer every email I receive.

If you liked the story, please write a short review for me on Amazon. I greatly appreciate any kind words, even one or two sentences go a long way. The number of reviews an ebook receives greatly improves how well an ebook does on Amazon.

Amazon – www.amazon.com/author/craigmartelle
Facebook – www.facebook.com/authorcraigmartelle
My web page – www.craigmartelle.com
Twitter – www.twitter.com/rick_banik

Thank you for reading the The Bad Company, the first book in an entire new series!

You know, how can I thank you for reading this story, and reading through the author notes if Craig has already beat me to it?

<Insert appropriate Marine comment here.>

One thing I will say I'm better at than I was a few decades before (I'm 50 as I write this.) I am aware of what I'm not good at, and what I don't think I will ever become good at doing.

Like writing post-apocalyptic fiction.

The challenge with that genre, is knowing how to actually *survive* and my idea of surviving is having to warm up a Totino's pizza in the microwave oven. Or worse, make fried cheese in the microwave oven...Ughhh.

So, you bet I reached out to speak with Craig. He was someone I was familiar with in the group and I just reached out and said 'can I talk with you?'

And there a friendship was made.

This last weekend (Nov 3-5th, 2017) here in Las Vegas,

Craig hosted the 20BooksTo50k Vegas conference. He was the show runner, the main speaker and THE GUY that put it on.

All I had to do was show up.

I've heard a lot of authors comment how well the conference went, how smoothly, how efficiently, and how nice everyone was to each other. Don't get me wrong, there were some complaints (too cold – Craig admitted he wanted it colder because warm rooms put people to sleep. I was never cold so I didn't notice.)

The conference was a non-profit effort Craig did to help other authors. That is just the kind of guy he is. Which, in a way, is why he writes Terry Henry Walton so well. Both are military guys who will kick your ass to get you moving, but help you get where you want to go and not ask for something in return.

Now, I have him chained in his office to write another 4,000 books (not really) and I expect him to come out of his office sometime in 2027 (this is mostly true.) I LOVE what is going on in the Space Opera field, so let me talk about THAT.

AGE OF EXPANSION

We (LMBPN Authors / Collaborators / Artists / Narrators) are a loose collective of creatives that enjoy working for and with each other. As these series progresses, the ability of us to provide YOU the fan with cool thoughts, stories, art, and other items depends on you sharing with US.

Meaning…

Love a character? Write us and tell us!

Love a ship and want to see it? Ask!

Want a short story on Audio? Share your thoughts!

We hope to help change a lot in Entertainment, and the way we keep creating cool and fun stuff is our fans encourage us (tell us on Facebook, mention it in reviews, tell friends etc. etc.) and just mention things that make you curious. What are those itches you want scratched?

How can we make something cool for you?

Hell if I know sometimes, but we HAVE taken suggestions, turned to an artist and said "I need XZY done because a fan wants to see it... When can we give it to them?"

Then, we meet in a seedy, smoke-filled bar where tennis shoes squeak while walking over the sticky alcohol splashed floor to exchange money for art under the table. The artist slips out the back under the light of a dirty incandescent lamp while we wait ten minutes, then throw a ten-dollar bill on the table and walk out the front.

Well, something like that. Perhaps it was a bit smokier than I'm letting on.

Either way, we LOVE to try and provide cool stuff and we will continue this effort.

We hope you enjoyed this story, and all of the stories coming at you in the next few months as we try to do something most companies wouldn't consider.

We want to produce one of the largest book shared Universes of Stories EVER done. I think we might be the biggest of all Indie groups, I don't know.

Anyone know the answer to this question?

I've read Warhammer has about 190 books (not including gaming modules) ... Star Wars is how many books?

I'm not including comic books at all for this discussion.

By summer, I think we should be at about 150 books in TKGU (The Kurtherian Gambit Universe.)

I wonder if Netflix would want to chat?

Oh well, if not no worries – we keep typing and hope you keep reading!

Ad Aeternitatem,
Michael

CONNECT WITH THE AUTHORS

Craig Martelle
Website: http://www.craigmartelle.com
Email List: http://www.craigmartelle.com/contact
Facebook Here:
https://www.facebook.com/AuthorCraigMartelle/
Email: Email: craig@craigmartelle.com

Michael Anderle
Website: http://kurtherianbooks.com/
Email List: http://kurtherianbooks.com/email-list/
Facebook Here:
https://www.facebook.com/TheKurtherianGambitBooks/

RICK BANIK THRILLERS

People Raged and the Sky Was on Fire (also on Audible)

The Heart Raged *Coming soon*

Paranoid in Paradise - a short story

SHORT STORIES (AND WHERE YOU CAN FIND THEM)

Earth Prime Anthology, Volume 1

(Stephen Lee & James M. Ward)

Apocalyptic Space Short Story Collection

(Stephen Lee & James M. Ward)

Lunar Resorts Anthology, Volume 2

(Stephen Lee & James M. Ward)

The Trenches of Centauri Prime

(in Galactic Frontiers, edited by Charles Ekeke)

The Misadventures of Jacob Wild McKilljoy

(with Michael-Scott Earle)

The Outcast (in Through the Never anthology):

Mystically Engineered

(in Tales from the Void, a Chris Fox Anthology)

A Language Barrier (in The Expanding Universe, Volume 3)

STANDALONE NOVELLAS

Just One More Fight

Wisdom's Journey

Fear Peace

BOX SETS & ANTHOLOGIES

Trader, Cygnus, & People Raged - Martelle Starter Library

The Expanding Universe, Volume 1 (edited by Craig Martelle)

The Expanding Universe, Volume 2 (edited by Craig Martelle)

The Expanding Universe, Volume 3 (edited by Craig Martelle)

Metamorphosis Alpha - Chronicles from the Warden Vol 1
(with James M. Ward, edited by Craig Martelle)

Metamorphosis Alpha - Chronicles from the Warden Vol 2
(with James M. Ward, edited by Craig Martelle) *Coming soon*

BOOKS BY MICHAEL ANDERLE

KURTHERIAN GAMBIT SERIES TITLES INCLUDE:

FIRST ARC

Death Becomes Her (01) - Queen Bitch (02) - Love Lost (03) -
Bite This (04) - Never Forsaken (05) - Under My Heel (06)
- Kneel Or Die (07)

SECOND ARC

We Will Build (08) - It's Hell To Choose (09) -
Release The Dogs of War (10) - Sued For Peace (11) -
We Have Contact (12) - My Ride is a Bitch (13) -
Don't Cross This Line (14)

THIRD ARC

Never Submit (15) - Never Surrender (16) - Forever Defend (17)
-

Might Makes Right (18) - Ahead Full (19) - Capture Death (20)
(2017) - Life Goes On (21) (2018)

THE SECOND DARK AGES

with Ell Leigh Clarke

The Dark Messiah (01) - The Darkest Night (02) -
Darkest Before The Dawn (03)

THE BORIS CHRONICLES

* with Paul C. Middleton *

Evacuation (1) - Retaliation (2) - Revelation (3) - *Coming soon*
Restitution

RECLAIMING HONOR

* with Justin Sloan*

Justice Is Calling (01) - Claimed By Honor (02) -

Judgement Has Fallen (03) - Angel of Reckoning (04) -

Born Into Flames (05) - Defending The Lost (06) - Saved By
Valor (07) -

Return of Victory (08)

THE ETHERIC ACADEMY

* with TS PAUL *

Alpha Class (01) - ALPHA CLASS - Engineering (02) -
Coming soon ALPHA CLASS (03)

TERRY HENRY "TH" WALTON CHRONICLES

* with Craig Martelle *

Nomad Found (01) - Nomad Redeemed (02) - Nomad Unleashed
(03) -

Nomad Supreme (04) - Nomad's Fury (05) - Nomad's Justice (06)
-

Nomad Avenged (07) - Nomad Mortis (08) - Nomad's Force (09)
-

Nomad's Galaxy (10)

PATH OF HEROES
with Brandon Barr
Rogue Mage (01)

A NEW DAWN
with Amy Hopkins
Dawn of Destiny (01) - Dawn of Darkness (02) -
Dawn of Deliverance (03)

~THE AGE OF EXPANSION~

THE ASCENSION MYTH
* with Ell Leigh Clarke *
Awakened (01) - Activated (02) - Called (03) - Sanctioned (04) -
Rebirth (05) - Retribution (06) - Cloaked (07) - Rogue Operator
(07.5)

CONFESSIONS OF A SPACE ANTHROPOLOGIST
* with Ell Leigh Clarke *
Giles Kurns: Rogue Operator (01)

THE UPRISE SAGE
* with Amy Duboff & Craig Martelle*
Covert Talents (01)

BAD COMPANY
* with Craig Martelle*
The Bad Company (01)

THE GHOST SQUADRON
* With Sarah Noffke and J.N. Chaney*

Formation (01)

OTHER BOOKS

With S.R. Russell

Etheric Recruit

with Craig Martelle & Justin Sloan

Gateway to the Universe

~THE REVELATIONS OF ORICERAN~

THE LEIRA CHRONICLES
with Martha Carr

Quest for Magic (0) - Waking Magic (1) - Release of Magic (2) -
Protection of Magic (3) - Rule of Magic (4)

SHORT STORIES

Frank Kurns Stories of the UnknownWorld 01 (7.5) *You Don't
Touch John's Cousin*

Frank Kurns Stories of the UnknownWorld 02 (9.5) *Bitch's
Night Out*

With Natalie Grey

Frank Kurns Stories of the Unknownworld 03 (13.25) *Bellatrix*

AUDIOBOOKS

Available at Amazon, Audible.com and iTunes

Made in United States
Orlando, FL
24 February 2023

30381358R00188